A Prin   *ry*

Also by Lindsay Clarke

SUNDAY WHITEMAN
THE CHYMICAL WEDDING
ALICE'S MASQUE
PARZIVAL AND THE STONE FROM HEAVEN
TRADITIONAL CELTIC STORIES
THE WATER THEATRE
A DANCE WITH HERMES
GREEN MAN DREAMING

A Prince Of Troy

LINDSAY CLARKE

HarperCollins*Publishers*

HarperCollins*Publishers* Ltd
1 London Bridge Street
London SE1 9GF

www.harpercollins.co.uk

First published as part of *The War at Troy* by HarperCollins*Publishers* 2004
This paperback edition 2020

A catalogue record for this book is available from the British Library

ISBN: 978-0-00-837104-3

Printed and bound in Great Britain by
CPI Group (UK) Ltd, Croydon CR0 4YY

MIX
Paper from
responsible sources
FSC® C007454

This book is produced from independently certified FSC™ paper
to ensure responsible forest management.

For more information visit: www.harpercollins.co.uk/green

For
Sean, Steve, Allen and Charlie

Contents

Map   viii

The Bard of Ithaca   1
The Apple of Discord   3
An Oracle of Fire   32
The Judgement of Paris   50
Priam's Son   64
A Horse for Poseidon   81
The Supplicant   104
The Trojan Embassy   131
The Madness of Aphrodite   147
The Flight from Sparta   172
A Perfect Case for War   187

Glossary of characters   193
Acknowledgements   199

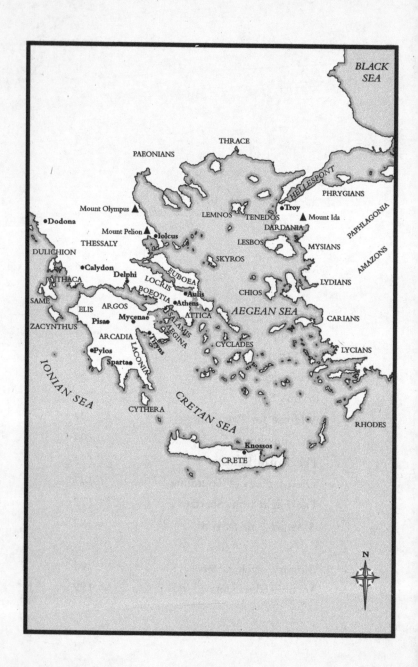

The Bard of Ithaca

In those days the realm of the gods lay closer to the world of men, and the gods were often seen to appear among us, sometimes manifesting as themselves, sometimes in human form, and sometimes in the form of animals. Also the people who lived at that time were closer to gods than we are and great deeds and marvels were much commoner then, which is why their stories are nobler and richer than our own. So that those stories should not pass from the earth, I have decided to set down all I have been told of the war at Troy — of the way it began, of the way it was fought, and of the way in which it was ended.

Today is a good day to begin. The sun stands at its zenith in the summer sky. When I lift my head I can hear the sound of lyres above the sea-swell, and voices singing in the town, and the beat of feet stamping in the dance. It is the feast day of Apollo. Forty years ago today, Odysseus returned to Ithaca, and I have good reason to recall that day for it was almost my last.

I was twenty years old, and all around me was blood and slaughter and the frenzy of a vengeful man. I can still see myself cowering beside the silver-studded throne. I remember the rank taste of fear in my mouth, the smell of blood in my nose, and when I close my eyes I see Odysseus standing over me, lifting his bloody sword.

Because Ares is not a god I serve, that feast of Apollo was the closest I have come — that I ever wish to come — to war. Yet the stories I have to tell are the tales of a war, and it was from Odysseus that I had them. How can that be? Because his son Telemachus saved me from the blind fury of Odysseus's sword by crying out that I was not among those who had sought to seize his wife and kingdom. So I was there, later, beside the hearth in the great hall of Ithaca, long after the frenzy had passed, when Odysseus told these stories to his son.

One day perhaps some other bard will do for Odysseus what I, Phemius of Ithaca, have failed to do and make a great song out of these stories, a song that men will sing for ever. Until that day, may a kind fate let what I set down stand as an honest man's memorial to the passions of both gods and men.

The Apple of Discord

The world is full of gods and no one can serve all of them. It is true, therefore, that a man's fate will hang upon the choices that he makes among the gods, and most accounts now say that the war at Troy began with such a choice when the Trojan hero Paris was summoned before the goddesses one hot afternoon on the high slopes of Mount Ida.

The Idaean Mountains stand some ten miles from the sea, across the River Scamander in that part of the kingdom of Troy which is known as Dardania. Odysseus assured me that an ancient cult of Phrygian Aphrodite existed among the Dardanian clan of Trojans at that time, and that as one of their chief herdsmen, Paris would have grown up in an atmosphere charged with the power of that seductive goddess. So it seems probable that he was gifted with a vision that brought him into her divine presence during the course of an initiatory ordeal on the summit of Mount Ida. But it is not permissible to speak directly of such secret rites, so we bards must employ imagination.

It began with a prickling sensation that he was being watched. Paris looked up from a pensive daydream and saw only his herd of grazing animals. They seemed, if anything, less alert than he was. Then, out of the corner of his eye, he caught a brief shimmering of light. When he turned his head, the trembling in the air shifted to the other side. Perplexed, Paris moved his gaze in that direction and heard a soft chuckle. Directly ahead of him in the dense shade of a pine, a male figure shivered into focus. Wearing a broad-brimmed travelling-hat and a light cloak draped across his slender form, he leaned against the trunk of the tree with the thumb of one hand tucked into his belt and holding a white-ribboned wand in the other. His head was tilted quizzically as though to appraise the herdsman's startled face.

Paris leapt to his feet, sensing that he was in the presence of a god.

A buzzard still glided through the sky's unsullied blue. The familiar view stretched below him to the rivers watering the plain of Troy. Yet it was as though he had stepped across a threshold of light into a more intense arena of awareness, for the feel of everything was altered. Even the air tasted thinner and sharper as though he had been lifted to a higher altitude. And it was the god Hermes who gestured with his staff.

'Zeus has commanded me to come. We need to talk, you and I.'

And with no sign of having moved at all, he was standing beside Paris, suggesting that they both recline on the grass while he explained his mission.

'Firstly,' Hermes said, 'you might care to examine this.' He took something shiny from the bag slung at his belt and handed it to Paris who looked down at the flash of sunlight from the golden apple that now lay in the palm of his hand. Turning it there, he ran his thumb over the words of an inscription and glanced back up at the god in bewilderment.

Hermes smiled. 'It says *To the Fairest*. Pretty, isn't it? But you wouldn't believe the trouble it's caused. That's what brings me here. We gods are in need of help, you see.' He took in the young man's puzzled frown. 'But none of this will make any sense to you unless I first tell you something of the story of Peleus.'

*　　*　　*

It's possible, I suppose, that it all started that way, though Odysseus always insisted that the war at Troy began where all wars begin – in the hearts and minds of mortal men. By then he had come to think of war as a dreadful patrimony passed on from one generation to the next, and he traced the seeds of the conflict back to the fathers of the men who fought those battles on the windy plain. Peleus was one of those fathers.

Odysseus himself was still a young man when he befriended Peleus, who had long been honoured as among the noblest souls in a generation of great Argive heroes. There had been a time too when Peleus had seemed, of all mortals, the one most favoured by the gods. Yet, much to his dismay, the young Ithacan adventurer found him to be a man of sorrows, prone to long fits of silent gloom over a life that had been shadowed by terrible losses. During the course of a single night Peleus told Odysseus as much of his story as he could bear to tell.

It began with a quarrel among three young men on the island of Aegina, a quarrel which ended with two of them in exile, and the other dead. Only just out of boyhood, Peleus and Telamon were the elder sons of Aeacus, a king renowned throughout all Argos and beyond for his great piety and justice. If Aeacus had a weakness it was that he favoured the youngest of his sons, a youth named Phocus, who had been born not to his wife, but to a priestess of the seal-cult on the island.

Displaced in their ageing father's affections, Peleus and Telamon nursed a lively dislike for this good-looking half-brother who was as sleek and muscular as the seal for which he was named, and excelled in all things, especially as an athlete. Their resentment turned to hatred when they began to suspect that Aeacus intended to name Phocus as his successor to the throne. Why else should he have been recalled to the island after he had voluntarily gone abroad to keep the peace? Certainly, the king's wife thought so, and she urged her own sons to look to their interests.

What happened next remains uncertain. We know that Telamon

and Peleus challenged their half-brother to a fivefold contest of athletics. We know that they emerged alive from that contest and that Phocus did not. We know too that the elder brothers claimed that his death was an accident – a stroke of ill luck when the stone discus thrown by Telamon went astray and struck him in the head. But there were also reports that there was more than one wound on the body, which was, in any case, found hidden in a wood.

Aeacus had no doubt of his sons' guilt, and both would have been killed if they had not realized their danger in time and fled the island. But the brothers then went separate ways, which leads me to believe that Peleus spoke the truth when he told his friend Odysseus that he had only reluctantly gone along with Telamon's plan to murder Phocus.

Whatever the case, when his father refused to listen to his claims of innocence, Telamon sought refuge on the island of Salamis, where he married the king's daughter and eventually succeeded to the throne. Peleus meanwhile fled northwards into Thessaly and found sanctuary there at the court of Actor, King of the Myrmidons.

Peleus was warmly welcomed by King Actor's son Eurytion. The two men quickly became friends, and when he learned what had happened on Aegina, Eurytion agreed to purify Peleus of the guilt of Phocus's death. Their friendship was sealed when Peleus was married to Eurytion's sister Polymela.

Not long after the wedding, reports came in of a great boar that was ravaging the cattle and crops of the neighbouring kingdom of Calydon. When Peleus heard that many of the greatest heroes of the age, including Theseus and Jason, were gathering to hunt down the boar, and that his brother Telamon would be numbered among them, he set out with Eurytion to join the chase.

Outside of warfare, there can rarely have been a more disastrous expedition than the hunt for the Calydonian boar. Because the king of that country had neglected to observe her rites, Divine Artemis had driven the boar mad, and it fought for its life with a fearful frenzy. By the time it was flushed into the open out of a densely thicketed stream, two men had already been killed, and a third hamstrung. An arrow was loosed by the virgin huntress Atalanta which struck the boar behind the ear. Telamon leapt forward with his boar-spear to finish the brute off, but he tripped on a tree-root and lost his footing. When Peleus rushed in to pull his brother to his feet, he looked up and saw the boar goring the guts out of another huntsman with its tusks. In too much haste, he hurled his javelin and saw it fly wide to lodge in the ribs of his friend Eurytion.

With two deaths on his conscience now, Peleus could not bear to face his bride Polymela or his friend's grieving father. So he retreated to the city of Iolcus with one of the other huntsmen, King Acastus, who offered to purify him of this new blood-guilt. But the shadows were still deepening around Peleus's life for while he was in Iolcus, Cretheis, the wife of Acastus, developed an unholy passion for him.

Embarrassed by her approaches, Peleus tried to fend her off, but when he rebuffed her more firmly, she sulked at first, and then her passion turned cruel. To avenge her humiliation, she sent word to Polymela that Peleus had forsaken her and intended to marry her own daughter. Two days later, having no idea what Cretheis had done, and assuming therefore that all the dreadful guilt of it was his, Peleus learned that his wife had hanged herself.

For a time he was out of his mind with grief. But his trials were not yet over. Alarmed by the consequences of her malice, Cretheis sought to cover her tracks by telling her husband that Peleus had tried to rape her. But having bound himself to Peleus in the rites of cleansing, Acastus had no wish to incur a sacrilegious blood-guilt of his own, so he took advice from his priests. Some time later he approached Peleus with a proposal.

'If you dwell on Polymela's death too long,' he said, 'you'll go mad from grief. Eurytion's death was an accident. In the confusion of the chase, it could have happened to anyone. And if your wife couldn't live with the thought of it, you are not to blame.

You must live your life, Peleus. You need air and light. How would it be if you and I took to the mountains again? If I challenged you to a hunting contest would you have the heart to rise to it?'

Thinking only that his friend meant well by him, Peleus seized the chance to get away from the pain of his blighted life. A hunting party was assembled. Taking spears and nets, and a belling pack of dogs, Peleus and Acastus set out at dawn for the high, forested crags of Mount Pelion. They hunted all day and at night they feasted under the stars. Relieved to be out there at altitude, in the uncomplicated world of male comradeship, Peleus drank too much of the heady wine they had brought, and fell into a stupor of bad dreams.

He woke in the damp chill of the early hours to find himself abandoned beside a burned-out fire, disarmed, and surrounded by a shaggy band of Centaur tribesmen who stank like their ponies and were arguing in their thick mountain speech over what to do with him. Some were for killing him there and then, but their leader – a young buck dressed in deerskins, with a bristling mane of chestnut hair – argued that there might be something to be learned from a man who had been cast out by the people of the city, and they decided to take him before their king. So Peleus was kicked to his feet and hustled upwards among steep falls of rock and scree, through gorse thickets and stands of oak and birch, across swiftly plunging cataracts, and on into a high gorge of the mountain that rang loud with falling water.

As the band approached with their prisoner, a group of women looked up from where they were beating skins against the flat stones of a stream and fell silent. The leader of the band climbed up a stairway of rocks and entered a cave half-way up a cliff-face. Kept waiting below, Peleus took in the stocky, untethered ponies that grazed a rough slope of grass. Goats stared at him from the rocks through black slotted eyes. He could see no sign of dwellings but patches of charred grass ringed with stones showed where fires were lit, and his nose was assailed by a pervasive smell of raw meat and rancid milk. Two children clad in goatskin smickets came to stand a few yards away. Their faces were stained with berry-juice. If he had moved suddenly, they would have shied like foals.

Eventually he was brought inside the cave where an old man with lank white hair, and shoulders gnarled and dark as olive wood, reclined on a pallet of leaves and deeply piled fresh grass. The air of the cave was made fragrant by the many bundles of medicinal herbs and simples hanging from its dry walls. The man gestured for Peleus to sit down beside him and silently offered him water from an earthenware jug. Then, wrinkling his eyes in a patient smile that seemed drawn from what felt like unfathomable depths of sadness, he spoke in the perfect, courtly accent of the Argive people. 'Tell me your story.'

Peleus later told Odysseus that he regained his sanity in his time among the Centaurs, but the truth is that he was lucky to fall into their hands at a moment when their king, Cheiron, was gravely concerned for the survival of his tribe.

The Centaurs had always been a reclusive, aboriginal people, living their own rough mountain life remote from the city dwellers and the farmers of the plain. Cheiron himself was renowned for his wisdom and healing powers and had, for many years, run a wilderness school in the mountains to which many kings used to send their sons for initiation at an early age. Pirithous, King of the Lapith people on the coast, had attended that school when he was a boy and always cherished fond memories of King Cheiron and his half-wild Centaurs. For that reason he invited them to come as guests to his wedding feast, but that day someone made the mistake of giving them wine to drink. The wine, to which their heads were quite unused, quickly maddened them. When they began to molest the women at the feast, a bloody fight broke out in which many people were killed and injured. Since that terrible day the tribe of Centaurs had been regarded by the uninitiated as less than human. Those who survived the battle at the feast fled to the mountains where men hunted them down like animals for sport.

By the time Peleus was brought before Cheiron in his cave there were very few of his people left. So during the long hours when they first talked, the two men came to recognize each other as noble souls who had suffered unjustly. At that moment Peleus had no desire to return to the world, so he accepted the offer gladly when Cheiron suggested that he might heal his wounded mind by living a simple life among the Centaurs for a time.

The days of that life proved strenuous, and in the nights Peleus was visited by vivid, disturbing dreams which Cheiron taught him how to read. He felt healed too by the music of the Centaurs, which seemed filled with the strains of wind and wild water yet had a haunting enchantment of its own. Through initiation into Cheiron's mysteries, Peleus rediscovered meaning in his world. And through his bond with Peleus, Cheiron began to hope that one day he might ensure the survival of his tribe by restoring good relations with the people of the cities below. So as well as friendship, the old man and the young man found hope in one another. That hope was strengthened one day when Peleus said that if he ever had a son, he would certainly send him to Cheiron for his education, and would encourage other princes to do the same.

'But first you must have a wife,' said Cheiron, and when he saw Pelion's face darken at the memory of Polymela, the old man stretched out a mottled hand. 'That dark time is past,' he said quietly, 'and a new life is opening for you. Several nights ago Sky-Father Zeus came to me in a dream and told me that it was time for my daughter to take a husband.'

Amazed to discover that Cheiron had a daughter, Peleus asked which one of the women of the tribe she might be. 'Thetis has not lived among us for a long time,' Cheiron answered. 'She followed her mother's ways and became a priestess of the cuttle-fish cult among the shore people, who honour her as an immortal goddess. She has given herself as daughter to the sea-god Nereus, but Zeus wants her and her cult must accept him. She is a woman of great beauty – though she has sworn never to marry unless she marries a god. In my dream, however, Zeus said that any son born to Thetis would prove to be even more powerful than his father, so she must be given to a mortal man.' Cheiron smiled. 'That man is you, my friend – though you must win her first. And to do that, you must undergo her rites and enter into her mystery.'

As with all mysteries, the true nature of the shore women's rites can be comprehended only by those who undergo them, so I can tell only what Odysseus told me of the account Peleus gave him of his first encounter with Thetis. It took place on a small island off the coast of Thessaly. Cheiron had advised him that his daughter was often carried across the strait on a dolphin's back. If Peleus concealed himself among the rocks, Thetis might be caught sleeping at mid-day in a sea-cave on the strand.

Following his mentor's instructions, Peleus crossed to the island, took cover behind a myrtle bush, and waited till the sun rose to its zenith. Then all his senses were ravished as he watched Thetis gliding towards the shore in the rainbow spume of spindrift blowing off the back of the dolphin she rode. Naked and glistening in the salt-light, she dismounted in the surf and waded ashore. He followed her at a distance, keeping out of sight, till she entered the narrow mouth of a sea-cave to shelter from the noonday sun.

Once sure she was asleep, he made his prayer to Zeus, lay down over her and clasped her body in a firm embrace. Thetis started awake at his touch, alarmed to find her limbs pinioned in the grip of a man. Immediately her body burst into flame. A torrent of fire licked round Peleus's arms, scorching his flesh and threatening to set his hair alight, but Cheiron had warned him that the nymph had acquired her sea-father's power of shape-shifting, and that he must not loosen his hold for a moment whatever dangerous form she took. So he grasped the figure of flame more tightly as Thetis writhed beneath him and took him on a fierce dance that wrestled him through all the elements.

When she saw that fire had failed to throw him, the nymph again changed shape. Peleus found himself floundering breathlessly as he clutched at the weight of water in a falling wave. His ears and lungs felt as though they were about to burst, but still he held on until the waters vanished and the hot maw of a ferocious lion was snarling up at him, only to be displaced in turn by a fanged serpent that hissed and twisted round him, viciously resisting his embrace. Then, under his exhausted gaze, the serpent took the shape of a giant cuttlefish, which sprayed a sticky gush of sepia ink over his face and body. Already burnt, half-drowned, mauled by fangs and talons, and almost blinded by the ink, Peleus was on the point of releasing his prize, when Thetis suddenly yielded to this resolute mortal who had withstood all her powers.

Gasping and breathless, Peleus looked down, saw the nymph resume her own beautiful form, and felt her body soften in his embrace. The embrace became more urgent and tender, and in the hour of passion that followed, the seed of their first son was sown.

The wedding-feast of Peleus and Thetis was celebrated at the full moon outside King Cheiron's cave in the high crags of Mount Pelion. It was the last occasion in the history of the world when all twelve immortal gods came down from Mount Olympus together to mingle happily with mortal men. A dozen golden thrones were set up for them on either side of the bride and groom. Sky-Father Zeus himself gave away the bride, and it was his wife Hera who lifted the bridal torch. The Three Fates attended the ceremony, and the Muses came to chant the nuptial hymns, while the fifty daughters of the sea-god Nereus twisted their line about the gorge in a spiral dance of celebration.

As their gift to Peleus, the Olympian gods presented him with a suit of armour made of shining gold, together with two immortal horses sired by the West Wind. King Cheiron gave the groom a matchless hunting spear, the head of which had been wrought by the lame god Hephaestus in his forge, while its ash-wood shaft had been cut and polished by the hands of Divine Athena. With the whole remaining tribe of Centaurs gathered in garlands for the occasion, and all the other revellers carousing on nectar served by Zeus's cup-bearer Ganymede, everyone agreed that there had been no more joyful marriage-feast since the Olympians had honoured the wedding of Cadmus and Harmony with their presence many years before.

Yet alone among the immortal gods, Eris had not been invited. Her name means *Strife* or *Discord,* and she is twin-sister to the war god Ares. Like him she delights in the fury and tumult of human conflict. It is Eris who stirs up trouble in the world by spreading rumours. She takes particular pleasure in the use of malicious gossip to create envy and jealousy, and for that reason none of the gods and goddesses other than her brother cares to have too much to do with her. For that same reason her name had been omitted from the list of guests at the wedding-feast of Peleus and Thetis. Yet all of the immortals have their place in the world and we ignore any of them at our peril.

Furious and slighted that she alone among the immortals had not been invited, Eris looked on at the festivities from the shadows of a nearby grove, waiting for the right moment to take her revenge. That moment came as Hera, Athene and Aphrodite were congratulating Peleus. The groom's eye was caught by a flash of light as something rolled towards him across the ground. All three of the goddesses exclaimed in wonder when he picked up a golden apple that lay glistening at his feet. With their curiosity excited by the goddesses' cries of delight, other guests quickly gathered round. Only Cheiron, to his dismay, saw the figure of Eris in her chequered robe slip away into the trees.

'Look', Peleus exclaimed, 'there's an inscription here.' Holding the apple to catch the light, he read aloud, '*To the Fairest.*' He turned to appraise the three goddesses standing beside him, and his smile instantly faded with the realization that he could not give the apple to any one of them without immediately offending the others.

'But I'm surrounded by beauty,' he prevaricated. 'This riddle is too hard.'

Aphrodite smiled at him. 'To the Fairest, you say? Then there's no difficulty. The apple must be meant for me.' The goddess was holding out her hand to take it when Hera said that as wife to Zeus, Lord of Olympus, there could hardly be any doubt that the apple should be hers.

'There is every possibility of doubt,' Athena put in. 'Any discriminating judge would agree that my claim to the apple is as strong as either of yours – if not a good deal stronger.'

Aphrodite laughed, dismissing Athena's claim as ridiculous. Who would look twice, she asked, at a goddess who insisted on wearing a helmet even to a wedding? Smiling in reparation, she conceded that Athena might be wiser than she was, and there was no doubting Hera's matronly virtue, but if beauty was the issue, then she had the advantage over both of them. Again, sidling closer to Peleus who stood in a consternation, wondering how he had got into this quandary and how to get out of it again, she held out her hand.

'Can't you see you're embarrassing our host, flaunting yourself like that with his bride looking on?' Athena protested. 'Perhaps one day you'll learn that true beauty is also modest.'

Sensing the imminence of an unseemly quarrel, Hera intervened, warning her divine sisters to restrain themselves. Then she smiled at Peleus and suggested that it would be best to settle the matter quickly by giving the apple to her. At which both the other goddesses turned on her, each clamouring to be heard over the other until all three were tangled in a rancorous exchange. The Muses faltered in their song, the Nereids ceased their dance, a nervous silence fell across the Centaurs, and the bride and groom looked on in dismay as the dispute became ever more acrimonious.

Hera spoke sharply above the others. 'If you two won't see reason, there's only one way to resolve the matter – Zeus must decide.' But neither of the others was about to accept that solution, nor did Almighty Zeus show any enthusiasm for it. Though he'd been drinking nectar all afternoon, he remained too astute to put himself in a position where his life would be made miserable by his wife if he was honest, or by two resentful goddesses if he was not. Hoping the row would peter out, he turned away. Only moments later, netted in a trance of rage, all three contenders began hurling insults at each other.

'Enough!' bellowed Zeus in a voice that briefly silenced everyone. 'If it's golden apples you want, all three of you can have a whole orchard of them any time you like.'

'It's not the apple!' Hera answered hotly. 'None of us cares about the apple!'

'Of course we don't,' Athena agreed.

'Then why are you embarrassing us all like this?' Zeus demanded. When no immediate answer came, he said it was time the goddesses remembered who they were and where they were. They should stop this bickering and sit down and enjoy themselves, so that everyone else could do the same. Again he tried to turn away but Aphrodite widened her eyes, protesting that the dispute was a matter of simple justice. She wasn't about to let some pretender lay claim to a title that everyone knew was rightly hers.

Sensing that her husband might be wavering, Hera hissed, 'Don't you dare take any notice of that mindless bitch.'

'And you shouldn't let your wife push you around,' Athena put in, 'not if you expect anyone ever to respect your judgement again.'

At which point Zeus shouted that he was damned if he would choose between them. Looking around in embarrassment, he turned back to the goddesses and said more quietly that, in his opinion, they were all beautiful. All three of them. Each in her own inimitable way. They should forget the apple and let that be an end to it.

'Things have gone too far for that,' said Hera. 'We demand a decision.'

Zeus met his wife's eyes with gloomy displeasure. For all his might, he could see no way of resolving this argument without causing endless resentment on Olympus. Yet when he shifted his gaze, it was only to see the assembled mortals staring at him, aghast and bewildered. Part of him already begrudged having ceded a nymph as beautiful as Thetis to a mere human. Now he was thinking that this trouble had come from mixing up the affairs of mortals and immortals, and when he caught himself thinking that way, he realized that Eris must be at the back of this quarrel and, if that was the case, there could be no reasonable solution. But the harm was done and he couldn't yet see how to undo it. Neither could he allow this disgraceful performance to carry on in front of mortal eyes.

'My decision,' he said at last, 'is that we shall return to Olympus immediately, and leave these good people to their feast.'

Moments later the immortals were back among the clouds on high Olympus. But when it quickly became clear that Zeus was still not prepared to make a judgement, the goddesses resumed their argument with uninhibited vehemence and no sign of a solution.

Meanwhile, having begun so joyfully, the wedding feast faltered to a dismal end. Thunderheads had been building over Pelion for some time and the gods had vanished in a livid flap of lightning. Now came the rain, and people ran for shelter, slipping among the rocks and stumbling about as though the storm had wrecked all expectations of peace and order in the world. As soon as the downpour eased, they made their apologies and dispersed back down the mountainside to their comfortable lives in the cities of the plain.

Dismayed that Sky Father Zeus had not been able to contain the fractious energy of the goddesses, Cheiron withdrew gloomily to his cave. The last time his Centaurs had attended a wedding-feast they had been depraved by wine and then hunted down like wolves. That had been the fault of men; but now it seemed even the gods had lost their senses. With the world so out of joint he decided that his people would keep to themselves from now on. If Peleus and his friends wanted to send their sons to be educated in the mountains, he would care for them, instruct them in music and the healing arts, and do what he could to set them on the path of wisdom. But with the gods at loggerheads, and most men's hearts no longer content with a simple, wilderness life such as he and his people led, he saw only dark omens for the future.

The years passed and things did not go well with the marriage of Peleus and Thetis. However uneasily, the couple had tried to laugh off the dismal fiasco of their wedding day, but it wasn't long before Peleus woke up to the fact that he knew almost nothing about his wife.

For a time, out there on the mountain, he had come to believe he might be happy once again. Exhilarated by his passionate encounter with Thetis, he began to be sure of it. They would make a good life together, raising children in the clear air of the mountains, far away from the ambitions and duplicity of the courtly world. But Thetis was a creature of the shore. She loved the salt-wind off the sea, the surge of a dolphin's back beneath her, the moonlit rush of surf, the smell of sea-wrack, the way the shingle tugged between her toes, and the marble world of rock pools. Up there in the mountains, she felt stranded. She pined for the long strands of sand and the sound of the sea, or raged with disgust and frustration at the horsy smell of the Centaur people and their stubborn, earth-bound ways. Having quarrelled with her father, and offended his chief tribesmen, she made it clear to Peleus that though they had been consigned to each other by Zeus himself, if he kept her in that gloomy mountain gorge against her will she would, quite simply, die.

Peleus already had a dead brother and a dead bride on his conscience. The first had been named for a seal and had also loved the sea. The second had hanged herself because instead of staying at her side, he had gone chasing a wild boar in the

Calydonian hills and killed her brother. The thought of another such death was more than he could bear. So he had already made up his mind that they would have to leave the mountain by the end of the summer, when a rider came looking for him out of Thessaly.

He brought the news that King Actor, who had never recovered from the loss of his son and his daughter, was now dead. The Myrmidons – those implacable soldier-ants of Thessaly – were now leaderless, and the messenger had been sent to ask Peleus to return and take up his rightful heritage as Actor's heir. He could be sure of a warm welcome, for some of the Myrmidons had been on the Calydonian boar-hunt and knew that Eurytion's death was an accident. Moreover the wife of Acastus had gone mad and had been heard boasting crazily that she was responsible for Polymela's suicide. In these circumstances, Peleus's right to rule would go unquestioned.

Here was a god-given answer to his problems. Both duty to his people and concern for his wife required him to leave the mountain. He would move the royal court from Athena's sanctuary in the inland city of Itonus down to one of the coastal strongholds. His wife would soon have the sound of the sea in her ears again. Thetis would be happy there.

Immediately Peleus set about making preparations for his return. Solemnly he said his farewells to the friends he had made among the Centaur people, promising that he would not forget them and that they would be welcomed as guests in his house should they ever want to come. Then he spent a long time alone with Cheiron, up on a windy shelf of rock high above the gorge, from where they could look out across all the summits of Thessaly and Magnesia to the eastern sea beyond. An eagle scaled the blue spaces about their heads. Everything else felt still and ancient round them. They were almost outside time up there, and watching the wind blow among the white locks of the old king's hair, Peleus knew that Cheiron was looking deeper into the heart of things than words could reach. And his own heart too was lost for speech – not because there was nothing to say but because there was too much. Yet in the silence of the mountain it felt as though it went understood.

After a time, Cheiron turned to look at him. 'You will do what you can for my people when I am gone?'

'It goes without saying. But you Centaurs live long. I think you have many years in you yet.'

'Perhaps.' Cheiron turned his face back to the wind. 'But my daughter,' he sighed. 'When I first spoke of her, I did not understand that she has immortal longings. A man will find it hard to live with that.'

Peleus frowned at the thought, and then made light of it. 'I'm not easy to live with myself. And Thetis will be content when we are by the sea.'

Again the Centaur said, 'Perhaps.'

The eagle glided high above them now, its pinions bent like a bow against the wind. Cheiron stared up at the way that strong span gleamed in flawless sunlight. Quietly he said, 'Remember that your son will be greater than you. Try not to resent him for it.'

'I shan't – because it will be your blood that makes him so. When he is of age I will send him to you.'

Cheiron nodded his old head. 'Then I shall live for that.'

Yet Thetis fell pregnant six times in the following years and each time she came to term, but not one of the infants lived for more than a week or two.

At each small death, Peleus found the sadness harder to bear, and all the more so because it was his wife's custom to withdraw to a sanctuary of the shore people between the start of her labour and the day when she hoped to present a living child to the world. When Peleus asked the reason for this practice, she told him it was a woman's mystery and not to be questioned.

Yet she returned each time, pallid and drawn, as if hollowed out by failure.

But she would say nothing more, so Peleus harboured his grief and returned to giving judgement in the world of men, and they lived a life that became ever more fraught with the silence that was left between them.

After the loss of the third child, he argued more strongly that it would be wise for them to consult her father who was more renowned for his medical knowledge than almost any man alive. But Thetis would not hear of it. She was a woman, she said, not a sick mare, and she wanted no truck with his mountain magic. Her trust was in her own understanding of these things as a sea-priestess to the moon-mother. In any case, had it not been prophesied that her son would be a stronger man than his father? Any child of hers that was not strong enough to survive the trials of birth had no place on the earth. He should not mourn them so.

Her ferocity astounded him, but he put it down in part to an effort to mask her own sorrow, and in part to the influence of the Dolopian priestess who was his wife's constant companion. A small, intense woman with deep-set eyes and a strawberry-birth mark shaped like a sea-horse on her neck, her name was Harpale. Thetis honoured her as a kinswoman, one of her mother's people, and she had begged Harpale to stay with her at the court of Peleus rather than joining her clan's recent migration to the island of Skyros.

The Dolopians were a restless people who had travelled from the far west a generation or two ago and settled about the shores of Thessaly. Now, under their king Lycomedes, some of them had felt the urge to move out to the Scattered Islands in the eastern sea and they had established a stronghold of their own on the windy island of Skyros. The move happened not long after Peleus had established his kingship over the Myrmidons, and feeling the strong call of island life, Thetis had wanted to go with them.

For a time it had been a struggle between them. Born on an island himself, Peleus knew the nature of the call, but he was king over a mainland people now and it was his wife's duty to remain with him and provide him with an heir. Was it not enough that he had already shifted the court to the coast for her sake?

He had understood her need for the sea. He was content for her to hold to cult practices which he did not share, and which – though he did not say it – he did not greatly trust. But she must respect the constraints imposed by royal duty on their life. They would remain where they were in Thessaly.

Meanwhile Peleus had been kept busy enough. Once he was secure on his throne he had harnessed the power of the Myrmidons to settle his score with Acastus. A swift, brutal campaign took them through Magnesia into Iolcus. Acastus was killed in the fight and his mad wife was quickly put to death. Giving thanks to Zeus and Artemis, who had a powerful cult centre in Iolcus, Peleus was declared king there and made Iolcus his new coastal capital.

Having learned the laws and customs of the Myrmidons, he set now about harmonizing them with those of Magnesia, trying to run a peaceable kingdom, and giving judgement in the quarrels with which his warlike men filled the boredom of their peaceful days. Also there was always a pressing need to raise money. To feed and clothe the royal households, to pay his retainers, arm his warriors, carry out his building projects, repair his ships, and make expensive offerings to the gods, all of this took a lot of gold. What could not be raised as tribute must be found elsewhere, so in company with the ageing Theseus, he turned pirate in the summer months and took to raiding the merchant ships and rich estates of the eastern seaboard.

He made his reputation as a valiant warrior and a generous king on those voyages, though his exploits never ranged as widely as those of his brother. Telamon had already sailed on Jason's *Argo* in the quest for the Golden Fleece, and had become a close comrade to Heracles, who was renowned and feared from Epirus to Paphlagonia as the boldest, most vigorous and, at times, the maddest hero of the age. Having already made a further expedition round the coast of the Black Sea into the land of the Amazons, Telamon and Heracles were now mounting a campaign against the Phrygian city of Troy.

Telamon tried to talk his brother into joining forces with them, but Peleus lacked his restless appetite for battle and was reluctant to risk his kingdom's hard won wealth in what promised to be an unprofitable attack on a bankrupt city recently visited by plague and earthquake. But neither did he wish to look weak in Telamon's eyes. In the end the decision was made for him by a wound he took in a ship-fight that spring. A Sidonian sword cut his right hamstring as he leapt aboard the galley, putting him out of action for months.

That was also the year in which his sixth child died in early infancy, and the grief of it was more than he could bear. A marriage that had begun so inauspiciously was now eroded by mutual disappointment, and its passion had faded as its tensions increased. Peleus was often given cause to puzzle over what Cheiron had said about Thetis entertaining immortal longings, but it seemed to account for her restlessness and the way her spirit sometimes chafed against his own more practical concerns. These days she seemed to take comfort only in Harpale's company, and Peleus grew to resent the power that the little Dolopian exercised over his wife's imagination. Harpale soon learned to stay out of his way, though her name frequently cropped up in conversation with his wife, reproaching him like the sting of a sea-urchin for the island life she was denied.

Of Thetis's failure to provide him with an heir it became ever harder to speak, so when he finally decided to consult Cheiron about his injured leg, Peleus went against his wife's wishes and raised this other, graver matter with him too.

Cheiron listened carefully as he applied thick poultices to his son-in-law's leg. He asked questions about the practices of the cuttlefish cult, and took a particular interest in the part that Harpale had come to play in his daughter's life. Knowing something of the Dolopians, he asked Peleus whether there had been any unusual signs of the use of fire in his daughter's rites. Peleus was unable to answer, however, because he was now excluded from all that part of his wife's life. His own service was to Zeus, to Apollo, and to the goddess, whether worshipped as Athena in Itonus or as Artemis in Iolcus; but as to his wife's most secret mysteries, he was as ignorant as his horse.

Cheiron nodded. 'Remain here till these herbs have shared their virtue. Had you come sooner I could have done more, but now you will always walk with a limp. Still,' he smiled up into his friend's face, 'if you had been your horse I would have had to cut your windpipe!' He fastened the bandage and sat back to wash his hands. 'As to the other matter, I will reflect on it.'

When Peleus travelled back down the mountain he brought with him a Centaur woman called Euhippe, who wept such fat tears when they left the gorge that Peleus guessed that the old king's pallet of grass would be a lonelier place after the parting. She was a small, round woman with a shyly attentive manner, and large, surprisingly delicate hands. Overtly she was to be taken into the household as a nurse for the care of Peleus's wound, but he soon intended to make it known that Euhippe was a skilful midwife too.

By the time he returned to his palace at Iolcus, Thetis was already over two months pregnant. Moody, and still prey to sickness, she at once made it clear that she would have nothing to do with the little mountain woman, whom she dismissed first as her father's hairy brood-mare, and then, after the cruel pretence of a closer look, as his jaded nag. Peleus protested. There was an unholy row between them that night, and silence for two weeks after.

Then the sickness passed, they talked and made love again, only to resume the queasy truce their life had become. Thetis still refused to include Euhippe among the women of her bed-chamber, but the Centaur found an unobtrusive place for herself in the royal household and her medical skills soon won her grateful friends. After successfully treating one woman for a rash around her midriff, and another for a dangerous fever, she gained a reputation as a wise woman and became a great favourite among the Myrmidon barons and their wives. Only Thetis, as her belly grew rounder by the month, continued to ignore her existence.

If she feared that Euhippe had been placed to spy on her, then her fears were justified, for on the occasions when she came to examine his leg, Peleus questioned her closely about anything she had learned of his wife's activities. For several weeks she found nothing unusual to report, but in the eighth month of Thetis's pregnancy, Euhippe made friends with a young woman who was complaining of intense pain from her monthly bleeding. Euhippe gave her a potion made up of guelder rose, skullcap and black haw for immediate relief, and advised her to return soon for further treatment. When she came back, they began to chat, and it emerged that the girl served as a handmaid in the cuttlefish cult. Through cautiously worded questions, Euhippe learned that there had been nothing outwardly wrong with any of Thetis's babies — no fevers or defects, nothing that would account for their early death. It was a mystery, the girl said, unless the Goddess had called them back to her.

When Euhippe asked her casually about Harpale's role in the cult, the girl flushed a little, looked away, and said that her own degree was lowly and she was too young to be initiated into such matters. Nor was she prepared to speculate.

'But there was a smell of fear about her,' Euhippe decided. 'She may not know much, but she knows more than she was letting on, and it frightens her.'

With his own suspicions now confirmed, Peleus asked Euhippe to keep her ears open, and eventually more emerged through one of the baron's wives. It was this woman who first dared to speak of witchcraft, but she did so darkly, casting her suspicions only on the Dolopian, not on Thetis herself, and in a way that left Euhippe feeling the woman meant her to report what she said.

Knowing that Thetis had once offended this woman, Peleus suggested that she might be spreading rumours out of spite, but Euhippe merely shrugged.

'You truly believe that something terrible is happening?' he demanded.

'For you it would be terrible,' she said.

'Do you know what it is?'

'I may be wrong.'

'Tell me anyway.'

Euhippe thought for a moment, then shook her head.

'Then what am I to think,' he demanded, 'what am I to do?'

'You need do nothing. Not until the baby is born.'

'And then?'

'Let us wait in patience. When the time comes we will see what to do.'

The truth of what happened at that time was known only to Peleus himself and he would not speak of it – not, that is, until some six years later when Odysseus arrived at his court for the first time. By then the child – Peleus's seventh son, and the only one to survive – was already in the mountains with Cheiron, learning how to live. Peleus lived alone in his gloomy palace under the patient, mostly silent care of Euhippe, and for a time his melancholic condition had been the talk of Argos. Telamon and Theseus had both tried to shake him out of it and failed. Cheiron was too old to come down from the mountains, and Peleus lacked the heart to seek him out. So the King of the Myrmidons wasted in his loneliness, limping from hall to chamber, hardly speaking, and increasingly reliant on trusted ministers to handle the affairs of state. Old friends like Pirithous and Theseus died. Power shifted south to Mycenae. People began to forget about him.

Then Odysseus ran his ship ashore on the strand at Iolcus. King Nestor of Pylos had encouraged him to come. Everyone responded to the lively young prince of Ithaca, he'd said – perhaps old Peleus might. 'Why not see if you can't tempt him to join you in your raid along the Mysian coast. Peleus was a good pirate in his day. He might be so again.'

There was, Odysseus quickly saw, no chance of it. The man could barely lift a smile let alone a sword. Shrugging his shoulders, he had made up his mind to cut his losses and push off at dawn, when Peleus looked up from his wine-cup for the first time in nearly an hour and said, 'It was good of you to come. Everyone has forgotten how to smile around me. You seem to do little else.'

'It costs me nothing,' Odysseus smiled. 'Does it disturb you?'

Unsmiling, Peleus shook his head. After a time he began to talk and a god must have entered him, for once he began it became unstoppable. That night witnessed a huge unburdening because Odysseus was the only person to whom Peleus ever spoke about what happened between himself and his wife. Odysseus listened in spellbound horror to a tormented account of how, at the prompting of Euhippe, he had cleansed himself before Zeus, begged forgiveness of the Goddess, and broken in to the sacred precinct around the sea-cave where Thetis held her rites. It was the dark of the moon after the birth of the child. Pushing aside the drug-intoxicated women who tried to stop him, Peleus entered the cave and saw the dark figures of Thetis and Harpale standing under a primitive wooden idol to the Goddess beside an altar of burning coals. Harpale held a finely meshed net of mail. Thetis was unwrapping the swaddling bands from her howling baby, and Peleus saw at once what they intended to do. If he had he not come in time to prevent it, she and Harpale would have done what they must have done many times before – they would have seined the child with fire, passing its tiny body back and forth along the shimmer of hot air above the altar's glowing coals until it was immortalized.

With a howl of execration, Peleus drew his sword, cut Harpale down where she stood, and snatched the baby from its screaming mother. Had the child not been squalling in his grip like a small storm, he might have killed Thetis also, but by the time he could lift the sword again the frenzied moment had passed and he could not bring himself to do it. Thetis saw the conflict in his face. Astoundingly, she released a small, frustrated laugh.

With the baby tussling in his arm, he stared at her as at a mad woman. She held his gaze, and they stood unmoving in the heat and sea-smell of the cave, knowing that the infant might have been spared its flames, but the fire that Thetis had lit had instantly consumed all traces of their love for one another.

Heart-broken, and unwilling to command the death of Cheiron's daughter, Peleus had her kept under close confinement for a time. The child he gave to a wet-nurse, one of Euhippe's friends, a Centaur woman who had been brought back from a hunt, freed at Peleus's insistence, and now lived with one of the palace cooks. It was she who named her tiny charge Achilles, the lipless one, because his lips had never been warmed into life at his mother's breast. But Peleus found it hard even to look at his son because the child's cries always recalled the horror of that night. On one thing, however, he was resolved — that Thetis should never come close either to the child or to himself. So in the end, on the understanding that she would die if ever she returned to Thessaly, he gave her leave to do what she had always wished to do and Thetis joined her mother's people on the remote island of Skyros.

'But the boy lived,' Odysseus said at last, filled with sympathy for the man who sat across from him, staring at the dying embers of the fire. 'You have a son and heir.'

'Whom I hardly know,' Peleus answered, 'and who knows nothing of me.'

'That can be repaired. You can recall him from Cheiron's school at any time.'

'To live in this darkness with me?'

'The child might lighten it.'

Sighing, Peleus searched the young Ithacan's face. 'Fortunately, it was prophesied that the boy will be a greater man than his father.'

Odysseus said, 'Then he will be a great soul indeed.'

★   ★   ★

Warmed by the company of this new friend, Peleus asked Odysseus to stay with him in Iolcus for a time. The Ithacan gladly agreed and the two men talked often together, exchanging stories of former exploits and discussing the changes in the world now that Agamemnon, the son of Atreus, had reclaimed the throne in Mycenae and was expanding his power to such an extent that he must soon be acclaimed as High King of all Argos. They talked of lighter matters too and Odysseus had at last got his host laughing merrily one evening when the arrival of another visitor was announced.

As a bastard son of King Actor, Menoetius was loosely related to Peleus by marriage, and he had sailed around the straits from the Locrian city of Opus in search of help from him. Menoetius had a six year old son who was in trouble, having killed one of his friends when an argument over a game of knucklebones turned into a fight.

'There's no great harm in the boy,' he said, frowning, 'apart from his passionate temper. And it breaks my heart, but I can't keep him with me in Opus. There's blood guilt on him now, and the father of the boy he killed loved his son as much as I do mine.'

Peleus nodded. 'So what are you asking of me?'

Menoetius asked if he might bring his son into the hall, and when permission was given, Peleus and Odysseus found themselves confronted by a scrawny six-year-old with a thick shock of hair and a downcast gaze firmly fixed on his own freshly scrubbed feet. Remembering how his own early fate had been shaped by the death of another, Peleus said, 'What's your name, boy?'

Briefly the small face glowered up at him in sulky defiance, then immediately looked down again, saying nothing.

'His name's Patroclus,' Menoetius said, 'though, as you see, he hasn't brought much glory on his father so far.'

'There's still plenty of time,' Odysseus put in lightly.

Menoetius looked back at Peleus in appeal. 'I hear that you've sent your own son to the Centaur?' When Peleus nodded again, he added. 'I was wondering if you thought he might be able to sort this boy out.'

'He sorted me out,' Peleus said quietly.

'But that dreadful business at the wedding of Pirithous . . . when they got drunk . . .' Menoetius saw Peleus frown. He hesitated and began again. 'I mean, weren't you already a man when you went to Cheiron.'

'I was more of a man when I came away. As were Pirithous and Jason, though they were sent to him as boys. And I might have been a better man still if I'd stayed among the Centaurs.' Peleus shook his head. 'But that was not my fate. As it is, I was glad to send my son to Cheiron. And since then a number of my Myrmidons have done the same.' He turned back to where Patroclus shifted uneasily on his feet. 'Look at me, boy.' Grimly, Patroclus did as he was bidden. 'Would you like to hunt and learn how to talk to horses? Would you like to know the magic locked in herbs, and how to sing and finger the lyre so that the animals come out of the trees to listen?'

Uncertainly Patroclus nodded.

'I think I'd like to go to this school myself,' Odysseus smiled.

Astounded by himself, Peleus said suddenly, 'Then come up the mountain with me tomorrow.'

Odysseus looked up, surprised at the transformation in his friend. Some god must be at work here. He felt the hairs prickle at the nape of his neck. But he smiled and nodded. Why not? Yes, he would be glad to go.

Peleus turned back to Menoetius. 'It's time I went to see how my own son's doing. You've done the right thing. Leave your boy with me.'

Apart from a tree that had been struck by lightning and the number of scruffy children to be fed, Peleus found the gorge hardly changed since the last time he had been there. But Cheiron felt much older, his cheeks were hollower than Peleus remembered, and the wrinkles deeply pouched about his eyes. His movements were slower too, though he was still limber, and his hands trembled as he offered a libation of mare's milk in thanksgiving for the return of his son and friend. He welcomed Odysseus warmly among his people, and smiled kindly at Patroclus, questioning him a little, before packing him off to play with some of the other children by the stream. A boy was sent to search for Achilles in the woods and, as they walked to the cave, Peleus explained why Patroclus had been sent to him. But Cheiron merely nodded in reply, and then shook his head over the way Peleus was limping across the rocks. 'You should have come to me sooner,' he said, 'then as now.'

As they ate together, Odysseus expressed his admiration for Cheiron's way of life. 'We still like to keep things simple on Ithaca,' he said. 'Some people find us rude and barbarous, yet we're honest and we have all we need there. It's only a restless lust for adventure that draws me away, but I'm always glad to get home again.'

Peleus sighed. 'I should never have left this place.'

'A man must follow his fate,' Cheiron said, 'and yours has been a hard one. I should have seen it sooner, but there are things the heart sees and will not believe.' Peleus insisted that none of the blame for his fate had been Cheiron's, but the old king gravely shook his head. 'Though she followed her mother's ways, Thetis is of my blood, and I have failed as a father.'

When Odysseus protested that Cheiron had been a good father to many of the greatest heroes of the age, the old Centaur sighed that a man could care well for the children of others yet be a fumbler with his own. 'It is only boys who come to me here,' he said, 'and though the power in the world may have passed to Sky-Father Zeus, the Goddess still has her claims to make on us – though sometimes it is hard for men to understand her mysteries.' He gazed up into the troubled eyes of Peleus and drew in his breath. 'But you have a fine son. He's already a skilful huntsman and he runs like the wind. Also he has a singing voice that will break your heart. You will be proud of Achilles – as he is already proud of you.' Cheiron took in the dubious tilt of Peleus's head. 'Oh yes, he knows that his father is a great king in Thessaly and has already taken a knock or two for bragging of it.'

At that moment all three men heard the eager, rowdy sound of boy's voices shouting in the gorge. They tried to resume their conversation, but the noise went on until Cheiron got up and said, 'It's time I put a stop to it.'

His guests followed him to the mouth of the cave where they looked down at the sward of rough grass among the rocks and saw two boys scrapping like fighting dogs inside a shifting circle of young, tousle-headed spectators who were urging them on. When they struggled back to their feet from where they had been flinging punches at each other on the ground, blood was bubbling from both their noses.

Peleus recognized Patroclus by the dark red tunic he was wearing. 'His father warned me that he had a bad temper, but this is a poor start. I trust the other fellow is strong enough to stand up to him.'

'I should think so,' Cheiron turned to him and smiled. 'He is your son.'

An Oracle of Fire

After the wedding-day of Peleus and Thetis a whole generation passed in the world of mortals, but the quarrel among the goddesses raged on and Zeus was no nearer to finding a solution. At last, out of all patience with the bitter atmosphere around him, he called a council among the gods, and Hermes, the shrewdest and most eloquent of the immortals, conceived of a possible way through.

It was obvious, he said, that none of the three goddesses would be satisfied until a judgement was made. It was equally clear that none of the immortals were in a position to choose among them without giving everlasting offence. Therefore it was his opinion that the decision should be placed in the hands of an impartial mortal.

Not at all displeased by the idea of returning the dispute to the mortal realm, Zeus asked if he had anyone particular in mind.

'I think,' smiled Hermes, 'that this is a matter for Paris to decide.'

Ares looked up at the mention of the name. That handsome bully of a god, who had come swaggering back from Thrace where they make war their sport and take as much delight in the lopping off of heads as others do in the finer points of art, had no doubt about which of the goddesses should be given the apple. He had long since grown bored therefore by a conflict that lacked real violence. Now he declared impatiently that Paris was an excellent choice. He knew him to be a fair-minded fellow with a good eye for the best fighting bulls in the Idaean Mountains.

Though she was restless to get back into the wilds, Artemis pointed out that being a bull fancier might not be the ideal qualification for the matter in hand. But before Hermes could respond, Ares went on to tell how Paris had once offered a crown as prize for any bull that could beat the champion he had raised. Just for the sport of it, Ares had transformed himself into a bull and thoroughly trounced Paris's beast. Yet even though the odds had been stacked against him, Paris had cheerfully awarded him the crown. So yes, Ares was quite sure of it – Paris could be relied on to give a fair judgement.

'I should perhaps add,' said Hermes, smiling amiably at the goddesses, who had, at that moment, no passionate interest in fighting bulls, 'that Paris is also the most handsome of mortal men.'

Zeus grunted at that. Sternly he looked back at the goddesses. 'Will all three of you be content to submit to this handsome mortal's judgement?' And when they nodded their assent, the lord of Olympus sighed with relief.

'Very well, Paris it shall be.' And asking Hermes to conduct the goddesses to Mount Ida, Zeus gratefully turned his thoughts to other matters.

As he sat in the sunlight watching his herd graze the pastures of Mount Ida, Paris was, of course, quite unaware that the gods had elected him to solve a problem that they could not solve themselves. But at that time he was ignorant of many other matters too, not least of the mystery of his own birth, for the youth entrusted with this awesome responsibility was rather more than the humble herdsman he believed himself to be.

Many years earlier, in the hours before he was born, his pregnant mother had woken in terror from a prophetic dream, and that dream was now beginning to cast a lurid light across the world. Yet as parents beget children, so one story begets another, and one cannot understand who Paris was without also knowing something about his parents, and something of his father's father too.

There were many Troys before the last Troy fell. One of them was ruled by a king called Laomedon, and the lore of the city tells how, as a humiliating punishment for displeasing Zeus, the gods Apollo and Poseidon were once forced to work for a year as day-labourers in that king's service. In return for a stipulated fee, Apollo played the lyre and tended Laomedon's flocks on Mount Ida while Poseidon toiled to build the walls around the city. Knowing that the walls would never fall unless some mortal was also involved in their construction, Poseidon delegated part of the work to Aeacus, who was the father of Peleus and Telamon. But Laomedon had a perfidious streak in his nature, and when the work was done he refused to make the agreed payment of all the cattle born in the kingdom during the course of that year.

It was not he but Zeus, he argued, who had put the gods to their tasks, and in any case what needs did the immortals have that they could not supply for themselves? So he turned them away from the city empty-handed.

The gods were not slow to take their revenge. In his aspect of a mouse-god, Apollo visited a plague upon Troy, while Earth-shaker Poseidon unleashed a huge sea-monster to terrorize its coastline. When a people already sickening from pestilence found their land made infertile by the huge breakers of salt-water that the monster set crashing across their fields, they demanded that Laomedon seek counsel from the oracle of Zeus as to how the gods might be appeased. The answer came that nothing less than the sacrifice of his beloved daughter Hesione would suffice.

Laomedon did all he could to resist the judgement, trying to force others in the city to offer their own daughters to the monster in Hesione's place. But the members of the Trojan assembly were fully aware that the king's perfidy was the cause of their grief, and would consent to no more than a casting of lots. In accordance with the will of the gods, the lot fell on Hesione. So Laomedon had to look on helplessly as his daughter was stripped of everything but her jewels, chained to a rock by the shore, and left alone to die.

The sea was rising and breaking round Hesione's naked body when she was found by Heracles as he returned with his friend Telamon from their expedition to the land of the Amazons. Using his prodigious strength, Heracles broke the chains and set Hesione free. But the sea-monster was still at large, so the hero struck a bargain with Laomedon, offering to put an end to the beast in return for two immortal white mares which were the pride of the king's herd.

The king accepted the offer and, after a fight that lasted for three terrible days, Heracles managed to kill the monster.

Once again Laomedon proved faithless. Ignoring the counsel of his son Podarces, he substituted mortal horses for the immortal mares that had been promised, and when Heracles discovered the deceit he declared war on Troy.

It was a war that left the city ravaged. As the son of Aeacus, Telamon was able to discover which part of Troy's walls had been built by his father and were, therefore, the weakest. He breached the city's defences at that place, Heracles joined him in the assault, and the palace was sacked. Driven by vengeful rage, Heracles killed Laomedon together with most of his family. Though Hesione's life was spared, she was given against her will to Telamon, and carried off by him to his stronghold on Salamis. But before she left Troy, Hesione was allowed to ransom the life of one other captive. The life she chose to save was that of her sole surviving brother, Podarces. It was he whom Heracles appointed as the king of a city reduced to smoking rubble. The new king was known ever afterwards as Priam, the ransomed one.

That anyway is how the story is told among the Trojan bards, and there were aspects of the tale that Telamon and Heracles were pleased to propagate among the Argives. But Odysseus was given a rather different version of the story by Telamon's brother Peleus. This is how he told it to me.

When they were boys, Telamon and Peleus had known for years of the longstanding feud between their father and King Laomedon of Troy. As a man widely known for his wisdom and skill, Aeacus had indeed been commissioned to rebuild and strengthen the ring wall around Troy. Because the city stood on a site prone to earthquakes, Aeacus entreated the divine help of Poseidon and those who understood his mysteries. He also brought with him a bard consecrated to Apollo. It was he who led the music which eased the men in the hard labour of carving, moving and lifting the great blocks of stone. The work went well. Lofty new gates guarded by bastions were built. The limestone blocks were skilfully laid to give a steeply angled batter to the lower part of the wall. Above it rose a gleaming crenellated parapet. So the new walls of Troy, rising from the windy hill above the plain, were both robust and beautiful.

Before the work was complete, however, it became clear that Laomedon was running short of money. When Aeacus saw that the king was unlikely to pay for the remainder of the work, he downed tools and returned to Salamis, leaving a stretch of the western wall unimproved and vulnerable. Eventually, infuriated by Laomedon's failure to come up with the money he was still owed, he called down the curses of Poseidon and Apollo on the city.

Many years later the Trojans were woken one morning by a dreadful sound. The waters of the bay between their two headlands were being sucked back towards the Hellespont, leaving the sea-bed exposed as a stinking marsh, strewn with rocks and slime and the carcasses of ancient ships. The ground under the city began to move. Buildings cracked, sagged and collapsed. People fled their houses as the sea came crashing back in a huge tumbling wall, higher than a house, that did not stop at the shore but rushed on to flood the fertile plain, destroying the harvest and salting the land.

Though the walls of Aeacus withstood the shock, the western defences and many houses inside the walls did not. Hundreds of lives were lost that day, trapped under fallen masonry or drowned by the wave. Soon a stench of decay polluted the city's air. Within a few days pestilence came.

Telamon and Heracles were caught in the turbulent waters as they sailed through the Black Sea into the Hellespont in the single ship that remained to them after their violent expedition to the land of the Amazons. By the time they sailed along the coast of Troy, the dirty weather had cleared and the waters calmed a little. But as they followed the shoreline, they were amazed to see a naked young woman bound to the rocks with the breakers surging round her.

The girl was half-dead from cold and fear, but Heracles cut her down, took her aboard ship and brought her round. She was not Princess Hesione, of course, for Laomedon had taken precautions to withhold his daughter's name from the lottery that had been held in the city. It was from the young woman on whom the lot had fallen that they learned of the city's desperate condition. Reduced to a primitive state of terror by their misfortunes, the Trojan people had resorted to human sacrifice to propitiate the gods.

Seeing an opportunity, Telamon sailed to Aegina and told his father that his curse had finally born fruit. If Aeacus would finance ten ships, he would return to Troy and take as plunder what had been withheld as payment. Aeacus agreed to put up only part of the money, so Telamon approached Peleus for the rest, but without success. In the end he and Heracles advanced against Troy with only six ships, but they carried enough men to breach the weakest part of the wall and sack the already devastated city.

In terms of hard coin and plunder, the expedition failed to make much profit, but Laomedon was killed and Telamon took his beautiful daughter Hesione as part of his share in the spoils. Priam's most prudent son, Podarces, only survived the slaughter when he ransomed his life by revealing where Laomedon had hidden what was left of his treasure. Before sailing away, Telamon placed a battered crown on the young Trojan's head and hailed him as King Priam.

Terrified, humiliated, but alive, Podarces swore to himself that he would wear the new name with pride, that he would do whatever was needed to redeem the fortunes of Troy, and that one day he would have his revenge on the barbarians from across the sea.

Before that time the Trojan people had tended to look westwards across the sea to Argos from where their ancestors had come in previous generations. The young King Priam now turned eastwards, opening up negotiations with the great bureaucratic regime of the Hittite empire, looking for loans to help him rebuild, and for trade to repay them. He met with a favourable response. Merchants of the Asian seaboard were also quick to see the advantages of a well-ruled city on a site commanding access to the Black Sea trade. Soon ships were putting in from Egypt too. New buildings began to rise inside the walls of Troy, not just new palaces and houses but also great weaving halls where the people were put to work manufacturing textiles from the raw materials that came into the city from the east as well as from their own mountain flocks. The Trojans' capacity for work became proverbial and the quality of that work was high, so trade profited. Beyond the city walls, Priam encouraged his people's traditional skills as horse-breakers until discriminating buyers began to look to Troy for their horses. And the king also took a particular delight in the powerful strain of bulls raised by his Dardanian kinsmen on the pastures of the Idaean Mountains.

Priam was not slow to thank the gods for the favour they had shown him. Soon after coming to the throne, he endowed an ancient mountain shrine to Apollo Smintheus, the bringer and healer of pestilence. Next he gave a new temple to the god inside the city, and then dedicated another on the sacred site at Thymbra. As his wealth increased, he built a spacious market square, surrounded by workshops and warehouses, and overlooked by a new temple which housed the Palladium, an ancient wooden image of the goddess standing only three cubits high that had been made by Pallas Athena herself, and on which the preservation of the city was said to depend.

Meanwhile the king had married. His wife Hecuba was the daughter of a Thracian king and their wedding sealed an important military and trading alliance. But there was also love between them, and Priam's happiness seemed complete when his queen gave birth to a strong son whom they named Hector because he was destined to be the mainstay of the city. Not long afterwards, Hecuba fell pregnant again and everything seemed set fair until a night shortly before the new child was due, when Hecuba woke in terror from an ominous dream.

In the dream she had given birth to a burning brand from which a spawn of fiery serpents swarmed until the entire city of Troy and all the forests of Mount Ida were ablaze. Disturbed by this dreadful oracle of fire, Priam summoned his soothsayer, who was the priest to Apollo at Thymbra and had the gift of interpreting dreams. The priest confirmed the king's fears – that if the child in Hecuba's womb was allowed to live, it would bring ruin on the city.

Two mornings later, the seer emerged from a prophetic trance to declare that a child would be born to a member of the royal house that day. Evil fortune would be averted only if both mother and child were put to death. To Priam's horror, Hecuba immediately went into labour.

Yet the queen was not the only pregnant woman in the royal household, and during the course of the morning, Priam received news that his sister Cilla had given birth to an infant son. Sick at heart, yet relieved to be spared the loss of his own wife and child, he commanded the immediate death of both his sister and her baby. Having seen the bodies buried in the sacred precinct of the city, Priam returned to his wife's chamber hopeful that the gods were now satisfied and the safety of his city assured.

But night had not yet fallen when Hecuba also gave birth to a son.

Priam looked up from the peaceful face of the child to see the priest and priestess of Apollo entering the bedchamber. He knew at once what was required of him, yet he could not bring himself to order these further and still closer deaths. 'Isn't it enough that one royal mother and her child have died today?' he demanded. 'Let the gods be content.'

Gravely the priest reminded him of the terrible fate that had fallen on Troy when his father Laomedon had tried to cheat the gods, and the priestess remained implacable in her conviction that the child at least must die. Had not Hecuba's own dream warned her that she carried the ruin of the city in her womb? Could it be wise to let it live at such dreadful cost?

'You have brought this evil into the world,' she said. 'Have the strength and wisdom to let it die by your own hand.'

When Hecuba could only wail out her refusal, the priest turned his gaze on the king. 'Will you risk all you have built for the sake of an ill-omened child?'

'I have served Apollo well,' Priam protested. 'How have I wronged him that he should persecute me so?'

The priest opened his hands. 'Apollo looks deep into the well of time. His concern is for the protection of this city.'

'If your kingdom is to live,' the priestess insisted, 'the child must die.'

'My sister and her newborn child are already dead at my command,' Priam cried. 'Would you have all the Furies roost in my mind? How much blood guilt do you think I can bear?'

The priest looked away. 'It's not we who demand this sacrifice. The king must choose between his city and the child.'

Looking for mercy where none was to be found, Priam lifted his eyes. 'Then let it be the child. But not at my wife's hand. And not at mine either.' He dragged the wailing infant from his wife's arms and gave it to the priestess. 'Do with it as you will,' he gasped, 'and leave us to our grief.'

With Hecuba screaming behind them, the priests left the chamber and handed over the baby to be killed by a palace guard. But the man could not bring himself to do the deed. When he consulted his friends, one of them said, 'Give the job to Agelaus. He's used to butchery.'

And so, hours later, in the village where he lived in the Dardanian mountains beyond the plain of Troy, the king's chief herdsman was drawn from sleep by a horseman hammering at his door. Told what was required of him, Agelaus looked down where the infant's swaddling bands were coming unwrapped.

'It seems a fine boy,' he said. 'Why does he have to die?'

'Because the king commands it,' the horseman replied.

Wondering why this unwanted task should have fallen to him, Agelaus shook his head. 'Did the king say by what means the child should die?'

'By any means you choose.' The man wheeled his mount to gallop away. 'This thing is the will of the gods,' he shouted over his shoulder. 'Be free of it.'

Though he had slaughtered countless animals in his time, Agelaus had no more stomach than the guard for cutting an infant's throat. Frowning down at the scrap of life in his arms, he muttered, 'If the gods think you should die, let the gods attend to it.' Then he took the child to a forest glade on the slopes of Mount Ida and left it there to perish or survive as fate decided.

Three days later, driven by his wife's insistence, the herdsman returned to the glade. When he saw the tracks of a bear headed that way, he expected to find nothing more than bloodied swaddling bands, but as he came closer a thin sound of crying drifted towards him on the breeze. Hurrying through the brakes, he found the baby still alive, bawling for food and almost blue with cold. Instantly his heart went out to it.

Holding the infant against his chest for warmth, he said, 'If the gods have sent a she-bear to suckle you, boy, they must mean you to live.' Tenderly, he placed the baby in the wallet slung at his side, and brought it home to his wife. It was she who spotted the birthmark like a kiss on the baby's neck and her heart was quickly lost to it. This child had been sent to them, she declared, and she would care for it. She named him Paris, which means 'wallet', because of the strange way in which he had come to her.

As the years went by, Paris soon distinguished himself both in courage and intelligence from the herdsmen round him. Even as a child he showed no fear among the bulls, and his greatest delight was to watch them fight one another and to see his own beast triumph. Under the patient tutelage of Agelaus, he soon proved himself a good huntsman and a skilful archer too. And he was still only ten years old on the day when he used his bow for a deadlier purpose than shooting wildfowl, though that had been his only intention when he took off into the woods.

The sun was thunderously hot that day and the air heavy. Paris had set out cheerfully enough but by early afternoon he was feeling drowsy and irritable. Casting about in the bracken for the arrows he had loosed and lost, he felt as though the thunder had got inside his head, so with only an old buck-rabbit and a partridge hanging at his belt, the boy was coming listlessly back down the hillside through the trees when he heard a restive sound of lowing from the cattle penned below.

Dismayed that his father had decided to move the herd without telling him, Paris was about to run down to join the drive when he heard men shouting – unfamiliar voices, strangely accented, barking out commands. He came to a halt while still under the cover of the trees and saw a gang of cattle-lifters breaking down a fence that Agelaus had built that spring.

He had counted nine of them, all armed with spears or swords, when more shouts drew his eyes to the right where Agelaus was running across the hillside from the settlement, followed by two of his herdsmen. They had no more than staves and a single hunting-spear between them. A burly man wearing a helmet and a studded leather jerkin advanced to meet them, drawing his sword and shouting to the others for support.

Paris's grip tightened on his bow. He saw that there were seven arrows left in his quiver. Swallowing, dry-mouthed, he took one of them between his fingers and nocked it to his bowstring.

By now six of the rustlers confronted Agelaus and his followers on the open meadow, and the other three were coming up quickly. As Agelaus grabbed the spear from the older man at his side, the helmeted leader brandished his sword and ordered one of his spearmen to throw. The man lifted his spear and was about to loose it when an arrow whistled out of the trees and pierced his neck. Herdsmen and rustlers alike watched in amazement as a gush of blood spluttered from his mouth, the spear fell from his hand and he crumpled to the ground. Seconds later, with a sparking of metal against metal, another arrow glanced off the leader's helmet. Taking advantage of the shock, Agelaus hurled his spear with such force that it drove through the jerkin and dragged the man down to the ground where he lay writhing and slobbering.

Again, for several moments, everyone stood transfixed.

A third arrow flew wide and stuck quivering in the grass. The rustlers had lost their leader but all three herdsmen were now weaponless with seven armed men standing only yards away. Paris loosed another shot at a scrawny rustler, who instantly dropped his spear to clutch at the shaft stuck in his thigh. The remaining cattle-lifters turned uncertainly, not knowing how many assailants were hidden in the trees. When a fourth man grunted and stared down to see an arrow trembling in his belly, three of the others started to run off down the hill. Moments later, unnerved as much by the unexpected alteration in their fortunes as by the groans of those dying around them, the others made off, stopping only to aid their injured comrade.

Agelaus and his companions were watching them hobble away down the hill when Paris came out from between the trees, carrying his bow. He heard his friends calling to him as if from a far distance. The air wobbled about his head. His throat was very dry. 'I had only two arrows left,' he mumbled as he fought free of Agelaus's embrace. Then he stood, looking down at where the dead leader lay with the spear-shaft through his lungs. Turning away in recoil, he saw the body of the man with the barb through his throat, and a third, who gazed up at him as if beseeching him to take back the arrow from his belly.

A nimbus of darkness circled behind the boy's eyes. He was watching the dying rustler choke on a gush of blood from his mouth when that dark circle widened and thickened so swiftly that it consumed all the light in the day.

He woke to the sound of water running over stones. He was beside a river in the shade of a thatched awning, lying on a litter, and the flash of white rapids came harsh against his eyes. The air about his head was aromatic with herbs. Savouring the mingled scents of balm, camomile and lavender, he moved his head and moaned a little at the dizziness. Then he saw the grey haired man sitting on a nearby rock, fingering the long curls of his beard.

A girl's voice said, 'I think he's awake.' Paris turned to look at her. 'Yes,' she cried, 'he is,' and her face broke into a bright, gap-toothed smile. Her hair also hung in curls, but so fair and fine they might have been spun from the light about her head. Wearing a white smock marked with grass stains, she was playing with a mouse that ran between her small hands. She was perhaps six years old. At her back, some distance away, were two grassy hummocks with stone portals, which looked like burial mounds.

'Bring him some water,' her father said, putting a gently restraining hand to the boy's shoulder. 'Lie still for a while,' he smiled. 'All will be well.'

Paris tilted his face to watch the girl as she stretched out to hold a drinking cup under a freshet of water bursting from a dark cleft in the rocks. The inside of his head felt burned out with pain. It was as though his violent dreams of fire and smoke and blazing buildings were still smouldering in there.

The girl came back and lifted the cup to his lips. 'You've been very sick, Alexander,' she said with the air of one endowed with privileged knowledge, 'but my father has the gift of healing. You'll soon be strong again.'

The water flowed across his tongue to break like light in his throat. He licked his parched lips, drank some more, then laid his head back. Struggling to retrieve the recent past, he remembered how the flies had gathered round the bloody wounds of the men he had slaughtered. His breath whimpered a little. Then he said, 'My name isn't Alexander.'

'No, it's Paris, I know. But you've been given another name since you drove off those cattle-lifters. They say you may only be a boy but you've become a defender of men, so that's what they call you now – Alexander. I like it better.'

'That's enough now,' her father said. 'Give him time to come to himself.' He smiled down at the boy again. 'I'm Apollo's priest at this shrine. My name's Cebren. Your father brought you here three days ago to be cured of the burning fever. He'll be glad to learn that the mouse-god has looked kindly on you. In two days he'll come to bring you home. All you need now is rest.'

'It's all right, Alexander,' the girl said. 'You needn't be afraid.'

'I'm not afraid.' Her arms were so thin they made him think of the stems of flowers. 'What's *your* name?' he asked.

'Oenone,' she answered. 'I'm the nymph of this fountain. One day I shall be a healer too.'

Paris smiled vaguely and, almost immediately, fell asleep again.

Agelaus came with a mule to carry his foster-son home bringing grateful offerings for the god and for the priest who served him. Received as a hero among his friends, Paris soon forgot how his mind had sickened at things he had done. In the years that followed, his boyish face developed the strong-lined, handsome features of a noble young man whose bodily strength had grown to match his courage. Renowned also for his good sense, he was often called upon for his counsel or to settle arguments among the herdsmen. So, as Agelaus aged and his muscles stiffened, Paris became the guardian of the herd, and out of love for the work he began to take an obsessive pride in breeding a formidable pedigree of fighting bulls.

Only once across the years was his chosen champion defeated in a fight. At that spring fair, a wild bull, blacker than a thundercloud, came down from the mountain, scattering the villagers and spreading alarm among the herd as it broke through the fence and began to storm and gore about the paddock. The bull fought with such ardour that Paris could only watch in astonishment while it bore down on his own favoured animal, trampled it under its hooves, and then twisted an immense horn through its breast to puncture the lungs. Though he was left aghast at the sight, the youth had no hesitation in honouring such ferocity with the victor's crown. Panting in its sweat, the bull quivered before him, tail swishing, black pelt splashed with blood. Paris gazed into the fierce roll of its eye. He heard someone mutter that the beast should be killed before it did more harm. Firmly he shook his head. 'No,' he entwined the crown of flowers about its horns, 'this bull goes free. Let him roam the mountains at his pleasure.'

Snorting in the dusty light, the bull dipped the blunt prow of its head as though in salute. Moments later, with the garland still gaily wreathed about its horns, it galloped back into the mountains.

When Agelaus remarked that never in all his long years as a herdsman had he seen a bull behave so strangely, Paris smiled and said, 'I think he was possessed by a god.'

At the spring fair two years later, Paris was garlanding the creamy-white curls of the bull he currently favoured, when he looked up and saw a young woman watching him from the edge of the trees across the paddock. Dappled sunlight shone off her hair. She was tall and lithe, and held a flower at her lips. All his senses instantly quickened to her presence. Then his heart jumped at the smile with which she studied him for a long moment. By the time she glanced modestly away he knew that never before had he seen anything so beautiful.

Unable to think of a sensible word to say, he crossed the few sunlit yards stretching between them and held out his hand to take the flower. Scarcely breathing, she watched him lift it to his lips. Then he strode back to where his bull panted in the afternoon light and twisted the stem into the garland already laid across its horns. Paris glanced back at the girl. 'Who are you? I don't recall having seen you before.'

Smiling she said, 'Perhaps if I had horns and a tail and snorted like a bull you would remember me.'

'I can't believe I would ever forget you.'

'But you clearly have,' she laughed. 'No doubt you will again.'

'Never. I swear it as I am a true man.'

She tilted her gaze away. 'Perhaps that is still to be proven – despite that leopard-skin you wear.'

He flushed at that. 'My name is Paris. No one doubts my courage. Or my faith.'

'I recall a boy whose bravery showed such promise,' she said. 'They called you Alexander then. You were a long sleeper in those days.'

Paris came closer, fixing her with a puzzled frown. The bright lilt of her voice brought the sound of water to his mind – white water, water over stones. 'You're the fountain nymph,' he said. 'From the shrine in the mountains. Your father healed me of the burning fever. You brought me water in a cup.'

'And you have never thought of me since!'

Again he flushed. 'You were only a child who played with a mouse.'

'While you were the great defender of men!' She laughed at his evident discomfiture, and then looked away into the trees, smiling still.

Not far from where they stood, the herdsmen and their wives were gathering under the awnings for the feast with children running noisily round them.

'Did you come down from the mountains to see the fair?' he asked. 'They say that King Anchises and his son will come to watch the games.'

'I came because the river told me to come.'

She glanced up at him. Their eyes might have been fixed on the same shaft of light. In a lower, less certain voice, she added, 'I have thought about you every day since then.'

Paris stood astonished as she turned away, back into the trees. Someone called out to him to join the feast. He raised a hand and answered that he would come soon. Then the girl's name came back to him. He whispered it to himself aloud: 'Oenone.'

But she was gone among the trees. Drawn by the thought that he could not let such beauty vanish from his life forever, he followed her into the green shades. She stopped when he called out her name. Timidly they talked for a time. Paris grew bolder. Laughing, Oenone turned away from him and ran deeper into the cover of the trees. He gave chase, following the sound of her laughter till he came out in a sunlit glade by the riverbank where the water sleeked its light through stones. It was there that she let herself be found.

Soon they were all but inseparable. Sometimes in the cool of the mornings they would hunt deer or wild boar together, traversing the mountain gorges where Paris carved Oenone's name into the bark of trees as loud torrents of melt-water cascaded down the rocks around them. And in the heat of the day they would often lie together in high alpine meadows that were bright with wild flowers as they watched the herds graze at their summer pasture.

Ignorant of his origins, free from all worldly cares, delighting in the strenuous country life which was all he had ever known, adored by his foster parents, admired by his friends, and deeply loved by Oenone, Paris might well have been considered as happy as a man can ever hope to be. Yet as the seasons passed a vague restlessness began to seize his soul. Not that he could have named it for himself, or that he was troubled by feelings of discontent;

but an obscure sense of horizons wider than that of the silent summits round him sometimes unsettled the reveries of the hours when he was alone. And it was on such an afternoon, while the heat was building over the high green pasture below the snow-line on Mount Ida, that fate ambushed him.

The Judgement of Paris

'So you see,' Hermes was saying, 'there'll be no peace till this argument is sorted out. We need an impartial judge to settle the issue and the general opinion was that you were the best man for the job.'

'Me?' Paris protested. 'How can a herdsman be expected to sort out a quarrel among the gods?'

Hermes tipped back the brim of his hat with his staff and cocked a wry eye at him. 'You have an eye for beauty, don't you? And Ares was impressed by your sense of justice. Anyway, the only thing the goddesses are agreed on is to abide by your decision. You should be flattered.'

But Paris was thinking quickly. 'How can I choose one of them without upsetting the others? Wouldn't it be simplest to divide the apple into three?'

'I'm afraid that none of the goddesses is prepared to compromise. It's gone too far for that. They want a decision.'

'Then I'm going to need your advice.'

Hermes held up his hands as though backing away. 'If I don't stay quite neutral my immortal life won't be worth living.'

'But I'm only human,' Paris protested, 'I'm bound to get it wrong.'

'Sooner or later every mortal has to make choices,' Hermes

said. 'This is your time. It's always a lonely moment but there's nothing to be done about that. If you're wise you'll assent to it. You never know, with three goddesses all eager for your good opinion, it might work out to your advantage.'

He tilted his head. 'Are you ready? Shall I summon them?'

As alarmed by the prospect ahead of him as he was strangely excited by it, Paris nodded. Hermes began to turn away, and then halted. 'One thing I will say. There's more at stake here than a golden apple.' Then he raised his staff and shook it so that the white ribbons flailed through the air.

Paris gasped as the three goddesses instantly appeared before him.

At the centre stood Hera, wearing her vine-wreathed crown from which dangled golden clusters of grapes. A shimmering, net-like robe embroidered with seeds and stars hung well on her shapely figure. She was, Paris saw at once, awesomely beautiful and entirely at ease in that relaxed kind of grace that knows its own power and has no need to make a show of it. With the poise of her regal authority, she acknowledged the wonder in his gaze.

To Hera's right, the more athletic Athena wore a light suit of finely crafted armour that was moulded to enhance her lissom form and the taut sinews of her slender limbs. In one hand she gripped a bronze-tipped spear, and in the other her aegis – the goatskin-covered shield on which a gorgon's head was depicted. It threw into contrast both the clear brilliance of her eyes and the grave, unclouded beauty of the face which studied Paris shrewdly now.

Aphrodite stood to Hera's left, leaning on one hip slightly to throw her form into relief beneath her simple, gauzy dress. She held her arms across her chest, with the palms of her hands pressed together and the tips of her fingers at her mouth. Violets were pinned in her hair and gilded flowers dangled from her ears. She tilted her head slightly to smile at Paris, then lowered her arms and watched the youth catch his breath as he took in the intricately-worked girdle that began as a necklace at her slender throat and curved down to separate and support the contours of her breasts.

Thinking she might have been too formal, Hera said, 'I see that Hermes didn't deceive us when he promised the most handsome mortal as our judge.'

Paris glanced away, gesturing towards his cattle. 'He's brought you a herdsman. One who's bound to make mistakes.' Still awestruck, he drew himself up to confront the goddesses. 'If I agree to make this judgement there have to be conditions.'

'Name them,' said Athena.

Paris took a deeper breath. 'All three of you have to forgive me in advance. Also I want an undertaking that none of you will harm me if the verdict goes against you.'

'That seems reasonable enough,' said Hera. Athena nodded. Aphrodite smiled and added, 'Very sensible too.'

'Then if you're all agreed to his terms,' said Hermes, 'we can proceed.' He looked back at Paris. 'Would you prefer to judge the contenders together or to examine each of them alone?'

Paris, who was having some difficulty keeping his eyes off Aphrodite's girdle, was about to reply, when Athena observed his air of distraction.

'I really must insist that Aphrodite takes off her *kestos,*' she said. 'We all know it makes men go weak at the knees.'

At once Aphrodite protested that her *kestos* was as much part of her own presentation as the heavenly crown was for Hera or Athena's armour was for her. When both the other goddesses dismissed her claim as preposterous, it seemed that the quarrel must break out again. Hermes was about to intervene but Paris, who had just begun to sense the power he might hold, lifted an imperious hand. 'I think its best if I see them one at a time,' he said. 'That way we should avoid arguments.'

'As you wish.'

'However, I don't see how we can avoid the suspicion of unfair advantage unless all the goddesses remove their jewellery and clothing.'

'You're the judge,' Hermes gravely replied. 'It's for you to set the rules.'

'Then let it be so.'

Hermes coughed. 'I believe you heard what Paris said. Would you kindly disrobe?' Turning discreetly away from the goddesses, he asked Paris in which order he would care to see the three contenders.

Paris thought for a moment. 'As Queen of Olympus, Divine Hera should take precedence. Then perhaps the Lady Athena, and lastly, Aphrodite.'

'Good luck then.' Hermes smiled.

And vanished.

Left in a state of agitation, Paris sat down. A moment later he was thinking, *Father Zeus forgive me*, as he found himself quite alone, staring at the Queen of Olympus who stood before him in all her naked majesty.

'You were quite wrong in what you said.' Hera turned so that the youth could admire the sweep of her back. 'You're rather more than a simple herdsman. Actually your birth is royal.' Turning again, she smiled down at his astonishment. 'King Priam is your true father. Go to his palace in Troy and announce yourself. Tell him the gods chose to spare your life. He'll rejoice to see you.'

Though the words astounded him, Paris experienced a jolt of recognition. Hadn't he always guessed at some such secret? Didn't it explain why he felt different from everybody round him? Didn't it account for his restlessness? With mounting excitement he listened as Hera told him the story of his birth.

'And there's more,' Hera smiled. 'You needn't be content with being a prince. Award me the prize today and you can be a king in your own right. I'll make you the mightiest sovereign in Asia. Wealth, empire and glory – all these can be yours. As Queen of Heaven and wife to Zeus, I can do this for you. You can be numbered among the wealthiest and most powerful of kings.'

Paris saw himself suddenly transported beyond the simple life of the hills into the teeming world of the cities – the world of

princes and palaces, of ministers, ambassadors and slaves, of im-
perial command and luxury such as even his father, the High
King of Troy, did not enjoy. How much might he achieve with
such power? What pleasures might such riches buy? Ambition
swelled inside him. He saw himself crowned and sceptred, sitting
on a jewelled throne with lesser kings obeisant before him and
Oenone as queen at his side. But the dissonance between such
grandeur and her simplicity unsettled him. He came to himself.
He stumbled out a reply. 'I shall always be grateful, Divine Hera
– both for revealing your beauty to me and for disclosing the
secret of my birth. If I find you the fairest of the three you shall
certainly have the apple. But . . .' he looked up at the goddess
and swallowed, 'my judgement is not for sale.'

The Queen of Olympus stared at his candid gaze for a long
moment without speaking. Tight-lipped, she nodded her head,
and disappeared.

Then Athena was standing before him, her vigorous body
gleaming as she turned. Everything about her appealed to his
hunter's senses, and when she faced him again, the serenity of
her clear gaze fell like sunlight on his soul.

'I suppose Hera has just tried to bribe you with power and
wealth,' she said. 'That's what matters to her. But there are more
important things, you know. Things which last longer and give
deeper satisfaction. If you want contentment then you'd better
get wisdom, and wisdom only comes from deep self-knowledge.
Without that everything else turns to dust.' The goddess moved
again to display her lithe form. The air around her strummed like
a lyre with kinetic energy. 'That's the deep law of things, and
though you may know *what* you are now, you still don't know
who you are.' Athena smiled down at him. 'So be wise today. Make
the right choice, and for the rest of your life you'll have me
beside you, both in war and peace, cultivating your wisdom,
protecting you in battle, and strengthening your soul until you
achieve perfect freedom and control. A mortal man can ask no
more.'

Paris nodded in silence, frowning and thoughtful. Vast new horizons were sweeping open within him. He had begun to understand that the choice to be made was not just between three modes of female beauty but between the deep, undying principles which shaped the values by which a man might live his life. Filled with a vertiginous sense of how his entire future destiny would be determined by his choice, he was trembling a little as he thanked Athena for sharing her beauty and wisdom with him. Then she was gone.

In her place stood Aphrodite.

For a long time the third goddess said nothing. There was, she knew, no need for words. Where Hera's regal confidence had steadied the air around the youth, and Athena had left it vibrant with her poise, Aphrodite filled it with a fragrance that excited all his senses. If outward beauty was the issue – he made up his mind at once – there was no contest. Only a few minutes earlier he would have beseeched Aphrodite to take the apple and do with him as she pleased. But his life had been changed in the past hour. He was no longer just a bull-boy free to while away his life in sunlight. He was a great king's son with a heritage to claim. He might be a man of moral and spiritual consequence. He had important things to think about.

Yet this third goddess was so dizzyingly beautiful that he could scarcely think at all.

'I know,' Aphrodite whispered, and there was a melting sadness in the eyes she lifted towards him – eyes of a blue such as he had previously glimpsed only at a far distance in the changing light off the sea. 'But it's not just about beauty any more, is it?'

'I'm not sure,' he said.

'I can see what's happened.' She looked away. 'The others have been offering you things. Tremendous things. Things you don't have. Things you hadn't even dreamed of.'

'Yes.'

'And I can only offer you love, which you already have, don't you?'

'Yes,' said Paris hoarsely, 'I do.'

But he was still considering the possibility that he might faint.

Aphrodite gave a rueful smile. 'Well, at least we can talk for a while.' She sat down with her legs drawn together, her elbows resting on her knees, and her face cupped in her hands, as though conceding that any further display of her beautiful body was pointless. Her eyes, however, remained deeply troubling.

Overwhelmed by her closeness, by the unselfconscious, naked presence of such heart-shaking beauty, Paris heard her say. 'She's lovely, isn't she? The fountain nymph, I mean.'

'Oenone.' He spoke the name almost wistfully, as if the friend and lover of his youth was already beginning to vanish beyond recall.

'I can see why she's so dear to you.' Like sunlight off a fountain, her smile flashed across at him. 'You're very lucky.'

Paris nodded. And swallowed.

'After all, she's given you the first unforgettable taste of what it's like to love and to be loved.'

'Yes.'

'So she'll always be dear to you, whatever happens.'

There was a silence, in which he realized he was barely sipping at the air.

After a time the goddess stirred and said, 'The world's so strange, isn't it? I mean, look at you – a simple herdsman one minute, a king's son the next, with the whole world at your feet. And here's me – one of the immortals, knowing that the apple is rightfully mine yet quite unable to claim it.' Again she sighed. 'I wouldn't normally be this patient, but you've been so good-natured about all this . . . and so honest with us! And I know that it can't be easy for you so I don't want you to feel badly about it. Anyway,' she gave him another regretful smile, 'I just want to say that it's been a real pleasure meeting you.'

But as soon as she began to move, Paris said, 'No, wait . . . please.'

The goddess tilted her head.

'I mean . . . what you said about Oenone. It's true, but . . .'

'But?'

'Well, only this afternoon, before all this happened, I was wondering . . . is that all there is? To love, I mean.'

The eyes of the goddess narrowed in a puzzled frown. 'You don't think it's enough?'

Paris frowned. 'It's not that.'

'Then what? I don't understand.'

He tried to gather his thoughts. 'I know what you mean. In fact, I've never been happier than since Oenone and I found each other. It's just that sometimes I feel . . .'

'Yes?'

He glanced up at her – 'that there might be more?' – then away again.

'More?'

Amazed by his own presumption, Paris decided to hold the goddess's searching gaze as he said, very quietly, 'Yes.'

With a shrug of her smooth shoulders Aphrodite gave a little, understanding laugh. 'Well, yes, there is, of course. There's a great deal more. But you seemed so happy as you are. I didn't think you'd want to know about it.'

'Tell me anyway.'

She sat back as if in mild surprise, puckering her lips. 'Well, it's not really the kind of thing you can *tell* anyone. It has to happen to you. You have to give yourself to it – you have to let yourself be taken.' She thought for a moment. 'It's like trusting yourself to the strength of the sea . . . and sometimes it's like giving yourself to a fire even.'

'A fire?'

'Oh yes. A fire so clear and intense that it burns away everything except the pure delight of its own passion. And once that happens then everything else changes. It all begins to make sense . . .' The goddess smiled and shook her head at the inadequacy of mere words. 'I thought you'd know rather more about it than you appear to do.'

The words had been added gently enough but they left him ruffled. He was on the point of claiming more knowledge than he had so far revealed but when he looked up into her comprehending smile he saw that such bluster would be immediately transparent. So he glanced away.

She said, 'So tell me more about these feelings you've been having.'

Suddenly aware how small those feelings seemed by contrast with the scale on which the goddess felt and thought, he flushed. 'They're hard to explain.' But his imagination seized on what she had said a moment earlier, and his heart jumped with a simultaneous sense of admission and betrayal as he added, 'It's as though once an experience starts to be familiar, it wants to change . . . to become something larger and more powerful. Stranger even.'

He looked for understanding in her eyes and found it there. She said, 'That's the unlived life inside you wanting to come out. You should listen to it.'

'I have been listening. I suppose that's why I'm here. In fact, I'm beginning to wonder whether . . .'

'Yes?'

He hesitated. Oenone's loving smile flashed before his eyes and vanished in the bright aura of Aphrodite's presence. 'What you were just talking about – do you think it could ever happen to me?'

'I'd like to think so, although . . .' She hesitated, pushed back a stray ringlet of hair, smiled, shook her head, glanced away.

'Go on.'

Aphrodite turned her searching eyes back to him. 'Are you sure you want me to?'

'Yes.' Swallowing again, he held her gaze. 'I'm quite sure.'

The goddess appeared to give the matter further thought. 'These things are always mysterious, you know. It's the *between*-ness, you see. It can't just happen with anyone. There has to be a meeting of souls. Souls that recognize each other. And when they do, there's a sudden astonishing freedom of both the feelings and the senses there that . . . well, that they just can't find with anybody else. It's the most tremendous experience of all, and it doesn't happen for everyone.' She tilted another rueful smile at him. 'So I'm afraid it's not only up to you.'

Paris nodded, and looked away.

'Oh I'm sorry,' she said. 'I shouldn't have said anything.'

'Yes you should. I needed to know about it.'

Quietly she said, 'But it hasn't happened with Oenone, has it?' And sighed when, frowning, he shook his head.

'Perhaps . . .' he began.

His throat felt parched as a summer gulch. He tried again.

'Perhaps she's not the right person. For me, I mean.' Looking up, he added quickly, 'Or me for her, of course.'

'Well, only you can know that for yourself. But . . .' She turned her gentle gaze on him again. 'You don't have a great deal of experience, do you? It must be hard for you to tell.'

A little humiliated by her sympathy, Paris watched as she glanced away, turned back towards him, opened her mouth to speak, and then appeared to change her mind.

'What were you going to say?' he pressed.

'I was just wondering whether . . . No, I really shouldn't interfere.'

'It's not interfering. I'd really like to hear what you have to say.'

'It's just that one of the advantages of being a goddess—' she smiled up at him '—is that we can see deeper into time than mortals can, and sometimes we're painfully aware of possibilities that you just don't seem to see.'

'You're thinking of me?'

As if making a difficult decision, Aphrodite drew in her breath. 'The thing is, Oenone is quite the sweetest creature in these mountains, but there are women in the world beside whom she's as simple and brown as one of my sparrows, and . . . Well, I don't think you've quite woken up yet to just how attractive you are, and how much power you might have over women – if only you gave yourself the chance to meet more of them.'

After a moment he said, 'You think there might be someone else for me?'

'I'm sure of it.'

'Do you know who?'

Aphrodite nodded.

'Are you going to tell me?'

The thought appeared to make her uncomfortable. 'I shouldn't really.'

Paris's eyes strayed towards the golden apple on the grass beside him.

'Oh no,' she exclaimed, holding up her hands. 'I'm not trying to bribe you. It's not like that. Now you've made *me* feel bad. Look, her name's Helen. She lives in Sparta.'

'Is that near Troy?'

'It's a kingdom in Argos.'

He frowned. 'I haven't heard of Argos either.'

'Argos is a country three hundred miles away. Across the sea.'

His face fell in disappointment. 'Then she couldn't possibly know about me.'

'Not yet. No.'

'And she's a foreigner.'

Aphrodite smiled. 'In love there are no foreigners.'

'But three hundred miles! And I've never been to sea.'

'So you don't want to know any more about her?'

'I didn't say that.'

There was another silence.

'Helen,' he said. 'It's a beautiful name.'

'It suits her. She's the most beautiful woman in the world.'

His eyes widened at that. 'Tell me more.'

'Wouldn't you rather see her? Yes? Then come and look into my eyes.'

Scarcely breathing, Paris moved until he was only a few inches away from the naked body of the goddess. She lifted her hands and cupped his cheeks. He trembled at the delicate pressure of her fingertips. Every pore of his body seemed to be taking in her fragrance as he lifted his eyes to meet hers.

And he was gone, vanished to himself, softly drowning in a sea-green iris of light, deeper than he would have thought his heart could take him, until he felt he was gazing upwards through blue fathoms at the dazzling surface beyond. Except that now he was suddenly looking downwards into the human face of a woman who gazed back up at him through the same compelling light – a woman to whom he was making love with a tender-ness and ardour such as he had never known. Hers was a face more luminous with passion and beauty than any he had ever seen before. It was as though, for those few timeless seconds, he was making love to the goddess herself, and even as the vision blurred he was feeling that, if it ever ended, his heart might die from yearning.

Then he was back on the mountain and the face smiling gently across at him was the face of Aphrodite.

'Helen,' she said simply.

Paris lowered his back against the grass and lay with his eyes closed, trying to hold on to the dream, savouring the exquisite pain of its loss. And yet, so intense was the memory, that he was filled with a fanatical conviction that, once having looked on that face, he could never forget it. Those eyes would be present to him each time he closed his own. There seemed no possibility that he would ever again dream any other dream than this.

Minutes passed. He was lost to the mountain, lost even to the presence of the goddess, and absolutely still – yet moving inwardly with a velocity that astonished him. Everything had changed. He could feel the blood pulsing through his veins. He could feel his heart blazing inside him. From this moment onwards, any instant of time less incandescent with life than this would not be life at all.

Without opening his eyes he said, 'I have to meet her. I have to make her mine.'

The goddess whispered, 'There's something else you should know.'

Eagerly he said, 'Yes?'

'Helen already has a husband.'

Paris sat up in shock.

Calmly she appraised his incredulous face. 'I know what you're thinking, and it's a problem, yes, but there are all kinds of things you don't understand yet.'

Outrage and betrayal darkened his eyes. Better never to have seen that face than to have looked on its beauty and have it snatched away like this.

'I understand well enough that she's already married, that she lives three hundred miles away in a place I've never heard of – and I suppose her husband's the King of Argos, right?'

'The King of Sparta actually.'

'So what chance have I got of winning her?'

'Without help,' she said quietly, 'probably none.'

But he was back inside the dream again. That face remained intimately alive inside him and indelibly present. It felt as inalienable as his soul. And the whole meaning of his life depended on it now. Surely it was unthinkable that a man should be gifted with such a vision unless it was possible to make it real?

Then he began to understand.

Clearing his throat, he said, 'What if you were to help me?'

Aphrodite pursed her lips in thought. 'It would be difficult.' She released a pensive sigh. 'And it might cause all kinds of trouble.'

'Suppose I gave you the apple in return?'

The goddess made a small offended grimace.

'It's rightly yours anyway,' he pressed.

'You're not just saying that because . . . ?'

'No, of course not. I wouldn't dream . . .'

She had glanced away. Now she looked back, unsmiling. 'Well, it could be done I suppose. But this is serious you understand? The matter of the heart is always serious – even when it looks like a game.' Her voice transfixed him.

'You would have to be sure that you really wanted her – whatever the cost.'

She allowed a moment for the thought to sink in. Then she said, 'Do you?'

He looked back into the solemn beauty of Aphrodite's face, and saw that the moment of choice had come. He glanced at the golden apple gleaming on the grass and saw that it was just as she had said – he had looked at Helen and everything had altered round him. Whatever else, he would never again be content to drive a dozy herd of cattle out to pasture and moon among the asphodels. He could no longer imagine what he would do with his life if he was denied the fulfilment of a desire that was now becoming an obsession.

Paris thought of everything he had been promised by the other goddesses. Hera would make him a great king, yes, but great kings had great troubles, and he was already a High King's son. Why should he want more wealth than that princely state would bring him? Athena had promised him wisdom and self-knowledge, but if he knew that the plain truth was that he wanted Helen, then wasn't that already self-knowledge enough? As for wisdom, surely that was as much a matter of the beating heart as of the intellect, and the vision of Helen had filled his heart with a fierce longing for the wilder reaches of love.

All the logic of the case pointed one way. Yet he looked up into the face of Aphrodite again and knew that none of that logic mattered to him in the least, for the truth lay far beyond logic in the hopeless, unrequited, irretrievable place from where, like a man passing sentence on himself, he said, 'I don't think I could live without her now.'

'Very well,' Aphrodite smiled. 'Give me the apple and I'll see what I can do.'

Priam's Son

Despite their earlier promise, Hera and Athena left the scene of their joint humiliation united in hostility both to Paris and to Troy. Happily, Paris was quite unaware of this, and Aphrodite was too delighted by her triumph to be troubled by her divine sisters' ill will. As a goddess never much concerned with moral consequence, she too had her powers. She would do what she could for the city – though it was hard to see how to preserve Troy from ruin while at the same time keeping her pledge to Paris. But to the latter task she was now utterly committed, and if a city had to burn as the price of passion, so be it.

Meanwhile, dazed with wonder and in the grip of obsession, Paris cared only that the loveliest of goddesses had promised to give him the most beautiful of women. He would not rest now until this destiny was fulfilled.

Night had fallen by the time he came down from the mountain.

Knowing that Oenone was puzzled by his distant manner, Paris retired without saying anything either to her or to his foster-parents about what had happened on Mount Ida. For much of the night he lay awake thinking about Helen and wondering how best to assert his true identity. Yet the gloom of his rough bothy was so far removed from the visionary presence of the goddess on the high mountainside that there were times when he found it hard to believe that the events of the afternoon had been anything more than a marvellous dream. A dream from which he had woken into a world grown small around him.

The next day, as always happened at that season, servants of King Priam came out of Troy to select from the herd a bull to be offered as prize in the funeral games that were held each year in memory of the king's lost son. Paris had often resented losing some of his finest breeding stock this way. Now he began to understand how his own fate had always been deeply bound up with that of the chosen beast.

Standing beside Agelaus, he watched the men from the city conferring over the bulls where they panted in the noon glare of the paddock. He already knew which one they would choose.

As he expected the leader of the party, a wall-eyed man with a curled beard shaped like a sickle, eventually nodded at him and said, 'Hobble me that white brute over there.' He was pointing to the bull that Paris had once garlanded for Oenone.

In previous years Paris would simply have jumped the rail and done as he was bidden. This time he studied the man steadily and said, 'Would you not rather take the skewbald bull beneath the oak? The eating will be as good and he will give you a deal less trouble on the road back to the city.'

The man turned his squint on Agelaus. 'The King commands only the best. He will take the white.'

'Then let the king hobble it himself,' said Paris, and walked away, with the hobbling-rope slung across his bare shoulder. Behind him he heard his foster-father stammering out bewildered words of apology. Then he saw Oenone watching from a plane-tree's shade. Involuntarily his eyes flinched away from her bewildered glance. He heard the bearded man saying that he had not come here to endure a yokel's insolence. Nor did he have all day to waste. Then he was ordering Agelaus to bring the bull out himself. When the old man began to climb the fence, Paris turned quickly on his heel, shouting to his father that the bull was too fast for him and not to be trusted.

'I was hobbling bulls before you were born, boy,' Agelaus growled, and leapt down into the paddock. 'Give me your rope.' One of the younger bulls let out a low, disgruntled bellow. The herd shifted nervously in the packed arena. Dust rose from their hooves. Already heavy with the smell of dung, the heat seemed to shimmer where dust drifted between the old man and his son.

Paris used his free hand to vault the fence. 'You're no longer as quick on your feet as you were. He'll gore you where you stand.'

Agelaus glared at him. 'Do you mean to insult me also?'

'No, father, but the truth is the truth. The bull is mine. He knows me. Leave him to me.'

'Are you forgetting that this whole herd belongs to King Priam?' said the bearded man, haughty and impatient. Paris stared at him for a moment, yielding nothing in pride or dignity, but it was to his foster-father that he said, 'Does King Priam always take such care to hold on to his own?' Then without waiting for an answer, he took the rope from his shoulder and advanced across the paddock to where, blinking among flies, with a tonnage of muscle twitching under its pelt, the chosen bull scraped a fore-hoof at the dust.

An hour later, as they watched the king's servants cart the tethered beast away, Agelaus said to his foster-son, 'Are you going to explain yourself?'

Paris said quietly, 'I mean to follow the bull to the king this year.'

'Has some demon got into you today?' the old man demanded. 'Is there not enough to do here among the bulls that you must go chasing trouble in Troy? Take a dip in the river, boy. Cool your head.' He was about to walk away, when Paris said, 'Tell me again about the time of my birth.'

Agelaus stopped in his tracks. He turned, frowning, and was slow to reply. 'You know the story well enough.'

'Tell me again.'

'It is as I said. I found you lying in the woods. A she-bear had suckled you there. I brought you home in my wallet and raised you as my own.'

Amazed that he had never thought to ask the question before, Paris said, 'Yet who among the Dardanians would dream of leaving a child alone to die?' When Agelaus glanced away, he spoke more firmly. 'Do you swear to me that you know nothing else?'

The old herdsman studied Paris gravely now. This was the first time the youth had directly challenged him, but he had always known that the question must come, and he was too honest a man to lie to the foster-son he loved. Drawing in his breath, he told Paris of the night when the king's horseman had come to the house, ordering him to kill the child, and how his heart had refused to obey. 'So instead of becoming your murderer, I became your father. Have you not been happy with us?' he demanded gruffly. 'What better life could you have wished for?'

'None,' Paris answered, 'except the life to which I was born.'

'And what if that life was cursed?'

'Whatever the case, at least that life would be my own.'

Paris saw the hurt in the old man's eyes. Immediately he regretted his own curt manner. 'You have always been a good father to me,' he said more gently, 'and I love you for it with all my heart. But a god has told me who my true father is, and there is a fate that comes with such knowledge.'

Remembering all the years during which he had watched the boy grow, Agelaus looked up into the noble features of the young stranger who stood before him now. 'Then who am I to argue with a god?' Biting his lip, he began to walk away, leaving the youth standing alone. But he had gone only a few yards when he stopped and stared down at the ground, shaking his grizzled head. Then he turned to look back at his disconsolate son. 'If fate requires it, go to Troy,' he said. 'Present yourself before the king.

Tell him that Agelaus gave you to the gods on Mount Ida and that the gods gave you back to me. Tell him that if there is fault in this, it is none of mine.' Then he turned again and walked away.

As Paris watched him go, he saw Oenone waiting for him in the plane tree's shade. The nymph had listened to the exchange with the same anxious foreboding that had kept her awake throughout the night, and she already knew that nothing she could say would deter Paris from his purpose. Feeling grief gather inside her now, she watched him approach across the glade.

Oenone listened in silence as he told her how a vision of Hera had come to him on Mount Ida and informed him of his true estate. Clenching her breath, she nodded when Paris asked if she understood why he must seek out the fate to which he was born. But when he promised that he would never forget the love that was between them, it was as though a louder noise was roaring inside her head. And when Paris lowered his mouth to kiss her, Oenone pulled back a little to fix his eyes with her own.

'I have the gift of prophecy from my father,' she whispered. 'I know that if I begged you to stay, you would still go out into the world, and I know that the world will do you harm. But my father gave me the gift of healing too.' She gazed up at him. 'One day you will take a wound that only I can heal. Come back to me then.' She reached up to kiss him swiftly on the mouth, then pulled free of his embrace and – as she had done once before, on the day that first made them lovers – Oenone ran from him into the shelter of the trees.

The drums were beating as he approached the city. The sound carried on the wind that swept over the plain of Troy, across the sheen of the rivers and through the swaying fields of wheat. From the distance he could see a large crowd gathered around the walls, shouting and cheering as they urged on the chariots racing there. He had often looked down from the mountains on the walls of Troy, but he had never seen them shine like this. Nor, he saw as he came closer, had he ever dreamed how massive those stones were, or how dauntingly high they stood. And he had never seen so many people before either – charioteers checking their axles and harness, athletes oiling their limbs, horse-breakers and farriers debating the merits of their mounts, acrobats and fire-eaters, snake-charmers, musicians and dancing girls, mountebanks and merchants, all looking to lighten the purses of the crowd, while among them beggars made a show of their sores and drunkards lolled among the women or snored beneath the makeshift stalls. The air smelled of spiced wine and charring meat, and the skin of his cheeks smarted at the sharp sting of dust blowing every-where on the wind.

No one took much notice of a farm-boy come down from the hills to mingle with the crowd and the youth was wondering how he would ever make his presence felt among this multitude when he heard a voice calling for more contenders in a bare-knuckle boxing championship. Approaching the ring of people, Paris recognized the young man at its centre as someone he had seen once before at the festival in Lyrnessus near the mountains. It was Aeneas, son of Anchises the King of the Dardanians, and though Paris had never spoken to the prince, he felt strength-ened by the sight of a familiar face.

For a time he stood by the ring of sand, watching as one fighter after another got knocked down by a muscular, sandy-haired youth in a scarlet kilt who, for all the weight of brawn he carried, danced nimbly on his feet and dealt out blackened eyes and bloody noses with contemptuous skill. Paris had no such talent with his fists, but he had learned to dodge and weave among the bulls, and to trust his own lithe sinews. Also he reck-oned he had a longer reach than the burly fellow who now calmly oiled his knuckles while his last opponent spat out a broken tooth. A party of girls were chanting out the winner's name. Deiphobus favoured them with a haughty smile as the umpire shouted, 'The King's son wins again. Does anyone else want to chance his arm?'

The tallest of the young women was already calling, 'Give him the crown, Aeneas,' when Paris stepped out of the crowd as if pushed by the unseen hand of a god. Somewhere he could hear the doleful bellow of his bull.

Aeneas grinned at him. 'Excellent, another challenger! And a Dardanian by the look of him. One of my own. But I shall strive to remain impartial.'

Paris had his eyes fixed on the muscular figure of Deiphobus where he stood laughing with the young women as he towelled himself. 'That is King Priam's son?' he asked, looking for something familiar in the youth's face and bearing.

'Deiphobus, yes.' Aeneas smiled. 'Is this your first time down from the hills?'

When Paris nodded one of the girls called out, 'Be gentle with the bull-boy, Deiphobus. It would be a shame to break that pretty nose.' A smaller, darker girl stood beside her, frowning at Paris with an air of puzzled hostility that he found slightly unnerving. But Deiphobus was ready to fight again. He stepped into the ring to loud applause from the crowd, measuring this fresh opponent with confident eyes. Then Paris was stripped to his breech-clout and standing across from him at the scratch-mark in the sand.

For a time Deiphobus sparred around him, flashing his fists in such swift jabs and feints that only Paris's agile movements prevented him from taking more than glancing blows. Growing impatient with the way this novice ducked and swerved, Deiphobus engaged him with concentrated aggression. More by luck than skill, Paris contrived to stay on his feet, and though his own blows hit only air, he was fresher than the other man and kept his wits about him. He had observed in the earlier fights how Deiphobus had a trick of pretending to drop his guard, then feinting to the left as he drove his right fist to the midriff, only to cut upwards with a rapid left to the head. He was waiting for that moment when it came. Deiphobus found his right thrust to the body parried by such a firm block that his own weight unbalanced him. Then his ears were ringing as Paris threw a stiff jab at his head. Paris closed quickly, pummelling at his opponent's body, and when he broke free of the clinch, he used his longer reach to crash a fist into his nose. Blood splashed. Deiphobus reeled, blinking for a few seconds. When Paris slammed him with another body-blow, his legs sagged under him and he was on his knees in the sand.

Amid the startled silence of the crowd, Paris leaned forward, offering a hand to pull him up. 'You fight well, brother,' he panted.

Scowling at what he took for a presumptuous insult, Deiphobus wiped the blood from his face, then brushed the proffered hand aside and staggered into the crowd. All the young women followed him except for the dark-eyed girl who stood for a moment, frowning at Paris as though she had seen him elsewhere and was still trying to place his face. But when he smiled at her she turned on her heel, darkening her frown, and hurried after the others.

'You fought well yourself,' said Aeneas. 'My cousin won't thank you for robbing him of this wreath.' Then he studied Paris more carefully. 'Weren't you at the fair in Lyrnessus last year? Didn't a bull of yours take first prize?' And when Paris nodded, his smile broadened. 'I thought so. It must have been the bulls who taught you to move as nimbly as that.'

'Deiphobus has more skill with his hands,' Paris said.

Aeneas warmed to the kind of openness that was commoner among the Dardanians than here in Troy. 'But you were a lot faster on your feet. Why not enter the footraces, friend? You might win yourself another crown.'

Three hours later Paris was summoned before the king where he sat among his courtiers in his gorgeously painted throne-room.

The rest of that afternoon had been a bright blur of heat and pace and building excitement. During the course of it, he had fallen foul of two more of Priam's sons by beating Antiphus in the dash and outstripping the people's favourite, Hector, in the cross-country race around the city walls. Now, with his blood running fast and high, he stood holding his three wreaths, tired and proud, and looking for the first time at the man who was his father.

'My nephew Aeneas tells me that you keep watch over my bulls in our Dardanian lands.' Priam stroked his perfumed beard as he gave Paris the distracted smile of a man who had carried the burdens of kingship for more than twenty years. Though he was in his middle-forties, Priam looked older. His thinning hair glistened towards silver and his gaunt face was creased with many lines. Yet he sat on his gilded throne with the air of one long familiar with its power as well as its cares, and when his eyes settled on Paris they left him more in awe at the king than eager to know more about his father. Only minutes earlier Priam had been given the news that a coastal town belonging to one of his allies had been pillaged and burned by yet another Argive raid. So as he fondled the ears of the boar-hound lying at his feet, the mind of the High King of Troy was still preoccupied with other things than a bull-boy come down from the hills to take the prizes at the games.

'It's not often a man wins a triple crown.' He gave a faint smile. 'Perhaps my sons would do well to pass more time in the mountain air?'

Holding his gaze, Paris answered, 'Perhaps they were lucky to have a father who did not expose them to the mountain air when they were born.'

'Was that your fate, boy?' Priam arched his brows. 'Well, I pity you for it. But it doesn't seem to have done you much harm. The gods must favour you. They have spared your life, given you a handsome enough face and the strength to make you winner of the games.' Priam glanced away, smiling at his counsellor Antenor. 'What more can a child of the mountain ask?'

'Nothing more,' Paris answered quietly, 'except his rightful heritage.'

Surprised how firm the voice, Priam looked sharply back at him. 'Which is?'

'To be acknowledged as your son.'

The King, his sons and the assembled courtiers were too astonished by the demand even to gasp. Before anyone could move or speak, Paris pressed on. 'I understand that these games are held in honour of the child you lost. Well, the child you lost has just won them. Those I have beaten are my brothers. I have come here to stake my life on the truth of this claim.'

At that moment the dark-haired girl who had been among the young women watching the boxing-match pushed her way forward between Hector and Antiphus. She had been staring at Paris ever since he had come into the hall and as soon as he had spoken, a familiar, tense pressure that was building inside her head broke like the release of lightning in a storm. 'Now I see you,' she said. 'You are the sacrifice that was not accepted.' She stood swaying on the balls of her feet. 'You are the brand that burns while my mother sleeps. There is the smell of smoke about you. I cannot breathe for it.' She turned to look at her father, white-faced. 'He will bring destruction on this city.'

'Be silent, Cassandra.' Impatiently, Priam signalled for some of the women of the palace to take the girl away, but Cassandra sought to resist them. 'He belongs to death,' she cried. 'He must be given back.'

Making the sign against the evil eye, Paris watched in dismay as the girl was hurried away out of the hall, but when he looked back at the people round him, they seemed less alarmed than embarrassed. Hector quickly stepped forward to cover that embarrassment. 'It looks as though the winner's wreath has gone to this bull-boy's head,' he laughed. 'He seems to have mistaken it for a royal crown.'

Some of the courtiers joined in the laughter, but Deiphobus, whose nose had been broken in the fight, was not amused. 'He has the air of a troublemaker. No one comes before the king and speaks as he has done. Who knows who he is, or what he has in mind?'

Antiphus said, 'Perhaps Cassandra is right for once? It might be as well to kill him anyway.'

Paris stiffened as a hostile murmur of assent gathered around him, but Aeneas stepped forward at his side. 'I think your sons are still nursing their bruises, Lord,' he suggested calmly. 'This youth beat them fairly in the games. I will attest to that. As to his other claims, only an honest man or a fool would stand before the High King and speak as he did. Might it not be as well to hear what he has to say?'

Priam considered a moment. Then he leaned forward to look more closely at the young man who stood before him, wary-eyed but unflinching. 'It's common knowledge that the gods once demanded a son of me. But that child was not given to the mountain.'

'Nevertheless your herdsman Agelaus left me there.'

'Yet you stand before me now.'

'A she-bear might have killed me but she suckled me instead.' Paris heard the sound of scoffing from where the king's sons stood, but his eyes were fixed on his father's eyes, where he discerned a glint of conflict between doubt and hope. He pressed on. 'When Agelaus found me unharmed, he lacked the heart to kill me – as did the horseman who had brought me from this city.'

Priam narrowed his eyes, unwilling to believe what he heard yet troubled by the pride and dignity with which this bull-boy withstood his gaze. He looked uncertainly to his counsellor, Antenor.

'Anyone might come before the king with such a story,' Antenor said. 'What proof do you have?' But before Paris could answer, a woman's voice rang from the open door of the throne-room. 'Let me see this youth.' Worn from much childbearing, and older than her years, Queen Hecuba walked through the parted crowd of courtiers with her hands clasped at her chest. She stopped a yard away from Paris and studied the young man with a gaze of such penetrating gravity that it would have shaken his soul had he not been given the goddesses' warranty for the truth of his claim. 'You have the long bones and the tilted eyes of a royal

Trojan, but so do many of my husband's by-blows. What proof do you have that you are the child of my loins?'

'Surely a mother should know her own son,' Paris answered quietly.

'Twenty years have passed since that child was torn from my arms. But its image is branded on my mind. There was a mark from the birth. It lay across my baby's neck. I remember thinking that it was as though he had been bitten by passion there.' The Queen's eyes gazed fiercely up at Paris. 'Do you have such a mark? Be sure you will die if you do not.' She beckoned Paris closer and reached up to lift the locks of wheat-coloured hair that fell across his left ear to his jaw-line. Paris tilted his head at his mother's touch. He heard the sharp catch of breath as she saw the mark's faint blush still blemishing his skin. Quickly she caught a hand to her mouth. A moment later her soft brow was pressed to his chest and he could feel her body shaking.

Priam rose from his throne. His queen glanced towards him, tears streaming down her cheeks. 'He carries the mark,' she said. 'This is our son.'

Over the long years of his reign, King Priam had coped with many shocks and surprises but none had shaken him like this. He stood, staring the impossible in the face, wanting to believe, yet not trusting that the same fate that had robbed him of a son could now so capriciously return him. 'You are sure?' he demanded hoarsely. 'It is not just your wish that speaks?'

'He has the mark, I tell you,' Hecuba cried. 'Come, embrace your son.'

But it was hard for Priam to look at the child whose life he had condemned. He closed his eyes and reached out a hand to support his weight against the throne. Then he was whispering to himself, 'The ways of the gods are not the ways of men, and what comes to pass is not always what was expected.'

With the dazed air of a man waking from a dream, King Priam opened his eyes and looked at the young champion holding his wreaths across from him. Then he raised himself to his full height, and opened his hands as though to catch invisible blessings falling from the sky. 'Let the ways of the gods be praised,' he said, and advanced to fold Paris in his arms.

With the astonished court looking on, King Priam held his lost son for a long time before he turned and said, 'My sons and daughters, come and embrace your lost brother. You must learn to love him as your mother and I already do.' Hector and the others stared uncertainly. The hall was loud with murmuring around them as, one by one, in obedience to their father's urging, the many brothers and sisters of Paris came to greet him.

Confident of his father's love, Hector, the oldest and noblest, stepped forward first to welcome his new-found brother warmly enough, but the feelings of the others were mixed and not always well concealed. Deiphobus replied with no more than a curt nod when Paris asked forgiveness for breaking his nose. Antiphus merely stared at him in scornful disbelief, and when Cassandra was brought back into the hall, she recoiled from Paris's anxious embrace as though her skin was scorching under his touch.

Only with his open-hearted cousin Aeneas did Paris feel completely at ease. It was he who guided the awe-struck youth through the labyrinth of painted apartments to a spacious bath-house, where slaves were summoned to bathe and massage him with perfumed oils, and dress his unruly hair. King Priam had commanded that the whole city should feast that night and Aeneas had undertaken to make sure that Paris would appear at the banquet garbed like a prince of Troy. But Paris had been troubled by the ungracious way in which most of his brothers and sisters had received him, and as he soaked in the bath, he shared his anxieties with Aeneas.

'It must be hard for them,' Aeneas answered. 'After all, only Hector is senior to you in birth, and it's obvious that you have a special place in the hearts of your parents. How could it be otherwise? It's bound to take time for the others to come round. But they have no real choice. Sooner or later they will.'

'You think that's true of Cassandra?'

'Ah! Cassandra is different. Cassandra is . . .' Aeneas hesitated.

'There's something wrong with her?'

'It's a strange story. She says that Apollo came to her one night while she slept in his temple at Thymbra. She says that he promised to give her the gift of prophecy if she would let him make love to her, and that when she withheld herself, the god grabbed her by the head and spat into her mouth so that no one would believe her prophecies.' Aeneas looked at his friend and shrugged.

'Do you believe her?' Paris asked.

'Do you believe what she said about you?'

'Of course not.'

Aeneas smiled. 'Neither does anyone else. It's all very sad. Cassandra is the most beautiful of your parents' daughters and she drives them to despair. But you mustn't let her gloomy nonsense bother you. Now come on. You're smelling more like a prince than a bull-boy now. It's time we found you some clothes to match.'

Aeneas helped Paris to choose among the selection of finely woven tunics and mantles that the butlers brought for his approval, and he advised him on a discreet choice from the jewellery casket, so that it was a true figure of a prince whose arrival was applauded when he joined the banquet that night. Paris was brought to a seat of honour between his parents. His father poured a grateful libation to the gods, and then asked the whole company to join him in drinking to the long life and good fortune of his handsome son.

Flattered, worried by his lack of social graces, and frankly bewildered by this abrupt alteration in his circumstances, Paris was soon aware that, wherever his own eyes turned, he was the object of curious attention. His heart was already dizzy with wave after wave of unfamiliar emotion. Soon his head was swimming like the dolphins and sea-horses painted on the walls around him.

During a pause in the feasting, Hector raised a drinking cup to toast him and called across the table, 'Andromache tells me you're already causing such a stir among the palace maidens that there's some risk they may come to blows if we don't quickly find a wife for you.'

Smiling with embarrassment, Paris acknowledged the jest. 'I thank your good lady, but tell her that I mean to sacrifice at the altar of Aphrodite every morning until the goddess brings me the one for whom my heart is fated.'

He did not miss the amused exchange of glances round him, and they left him discomfited. He saw that he would have to learn to be less open among these clever, cultivated men and the painted women in their costly garments who left him feeling boyish and awkward. With a pang of regret, he thought about Oenone and the simple mountain life they had lived together. His heart quailed for a moment. But then his mother Hecuba was leaning towards him. 'My son considers himself a servant of Aphrodite?'

'I do, madam.'

Priam looked up from where he had been lost in thought and smiled across at Paris. 'It seems that they made a Dardanian of you out there on the mountains. The Golden One is greatly revered by Anchises and his people.'

Hector said, 'Then it's small wonder that you and Aeneas should be friends. I understand that in Lyrnessus they say that Aphrodite is his mother.' He turned, smiling archly, to Aeneas. 'Isn't that so, son of Anchises?'

Well used to the jibe, Aeneas raised his cup to him, and smiled at the astonishment on his friend's face, for though Aphrodite had not been far from Paris's mind in the past few hours, he had never for a moment thought of her as a mother. 'I was sired in Aphrodite's temple,' Aeneas explained. 'My mother was her priestess.'

'But the story is more colourful,' said Priam. 'Have you not heard it, Paris – how my cousin Anchises was blinded by the goddess for bragging of her love for him? Where is my bard? Let us have the song.'

The bard, who had been chattering among the ladies of the

court, reached for his lyre and began to play. As the chords thrilled across the air of the hall, the feasters fell silent. The bard lifted his voice and began to sing of how Zeus had once decided to humble Aphrodite by making her fall in love with a mere mortal. He made the heart of the goddess burn with such ardour for the young Anchises that she appeared before him in a stable disguised as a Phrygian princess and wearing a robe more brilliant than flames of fire. Aphrodite gave herself to him in a night of tremendous passion, but Anchises shook with terror when he woke in the dawn light to find that it wasn't a naked woman he held in his arms but an immortal goddess. Aphrodite told him that he need fear nothing so long as he preserved the secret of their love, but his heart was so full with the knowledge that he was bursting to make it known. When he did so, he was blinded by a thunderbolt.

Paris had heard neither the song nor the story before. It was more courtly and sophisticated than the country songs he used to sing with his friends in the mountains, and there was a wry edge to the words that left him wondering whether both Aphrodite and Anchises were being mocked by the bard. But Aeneas seemed to take it all in good part, so Paris relaxed and joined in the applause when the lay was ended.

Hecuba placed a mottled hand across his own. 'Golden Aphrodite can be a gentle goddess,' she said, 'but she is also ruthless. Perhaps you are a child of passion after all, but take care that her service does not consume you.'

'Your mother speaks wisely,' Priam nodded. 'It's best that a man tries to honour all the gods – though there are times when it seems they have little care for us.'

Looking earnestly back at his parents, Paris saw how, even in this hour of celebration, difficult questions of state still troubled his father's mind. He felt suddenly glad that he had refused Hera's offer of a kingly throne. And when he studied his mother he could see the strength of Hera in her matronly grace, and he could hear something of Athena's wisdom in her words. But the memory of Aphrodite's fragrance assailed his senses in the heady scent of lilies from the banquet table, in the way a serving-girl casually brushed against him as she filled his goblet with wine, and in the vivid eyes that reached out to him across the room, brightened a moment, and swiftly darted away. For better or worse, he belonged entirely to the Golden One now.

'I thank you both for your care,' he answered, smiling, 'but my vow was made before I came and I trust to Aphrodite's divine protection.' He took a deep draught from the cup of spiced wine he had raised. 'Believe me, if it is my fate to be consumed by beauty, I shall go to meet it with an eager heart.'

A Horse for Poseidon

A man must make his choices but to a god almost all things are possible. Thus when amorous Zeus takes a fancy to a woman he has many means of ensuring his desire is gratified. Once, having set eyes on Europa while she sported on the shore, he took the form of a bull and behaved so tamely before her that she dared to mount his massive back. A moment later the girl was carried through the breakers, out across the open sea to Crete, where the god took pleasure in planting the seed of Minos in her loins. Again, when Zeus came across the moon-maiden Danae shut inside a brazen tower where she had been imprisoned by her father, the god dissolved into a shower of gold, and through his incandescent act of lust the hero Perseus was conceived.

But the most momentous of his changes happened one fateful day when the Sky-Father saw the wife of Tyndareus, King of Sparta, bathing naked and alone in the river Eurotas. Inflamed by passion, he plumed his mighty form into a swan and bore down on her with his strong neck and white wings. Lacking strength or time to resist the god's sudden swoop, Leda was taken, gasping, into his embrace. When he was done, and his need satisfied, Zeus flew away, leaving her pregnant with the deaths of thousands of men, for it was Helen who was sired by this rape.

So graceful and delicate was the blush of beauty on the child that men said she had truly been hatched from the egg of a divine swan. But Leda had lain with her husband earlier that night, so when Helen was born, Tyndareus chose to raise her as his own child at the Spartan court. Not long afterwards, drawn by the god who had taken possession both of her body and her soul, Leda left Sparta and travelled northwards to the oak forest of Dodona where she gave herself in an ascetic life of prophetic service to Zeus.

Meanwhile, as the child grew, so did the rumour of her beauty until men everywhere began dreaming that one day Helen might be theirs. But Tyndareus had another, older daughter, one who found it hard to endure the way that Helen's poise and grace, those sea-green eyes and the long black fall of hair, consumed all the attention in a room the moment she entered it. Her name was Clytaemnestra, and though she was considered pretty in her own way, she had to learn from an early age that she must live in the shadow cast by the radiance of her younger sister's face. And what came hardest was the knowledge that even her father was infatuated by Helen's beauty, so there was little sisterly affection between the two girls.

Helen's delight was to be out in the sunlight, swimming in the Eurotas, or testing her slender body as an athlete among the other young men and women of Sparta. Above all things she loved to venture into lonely stretches of wilderness, discovering hidden springs or hunting with her bow in the wooded mountains that ringed the Laconian plain. Perhaps to console herself for the early loss of her mother, she developed a strong affinity for animals, and on one occasion – she was only eight years old at the time – she caused a great consternation among the huntsmen when they found her on a craggy outcrop, fondling the cubs of a mountain lion while their mother licked her huge paws on a sunlit rock nearby. Soon afterwards she became a devotee of the Virgin Artemis and could often be found singing hymns to the goddess in some wild shrine or leading the maidens of Sparta in her dance.

By contrast, Clytaemnestra rarely left the grounds of the palace, and tried to win her father's attention by taking an interest in the politics of his kingdom and his negotiations with ambassadors from other lands. When Tyndareus made it clear that her opinions were unwelcome, she withdrew into a studious world of her own where she developed a sharp, disputatious intellect, arguing over the interpretation of oracles with the priests, evolving a sharp-eyed pragmatic philosophy of her own, and dreaming of a time when a man of her choice would look her way rather than nursing fantasies of Helen.

One young man had already shown such a preference, but he was a big, coarse-grained, moody fellow of no great intelligence and not to her taste. He was one of two brothers who had fled to Sparta after their father Atreus was killed in the struggle for control of Mycenae, and the cast of his mind had been darkened by the bloody events he had survived. As was usually the case, the younger brother, Menelaus, soon began to moon over Helen's beauty, but the elder brother, Agamemnon, was drawn to the sullen fire he sensed burning in Clytaemnestra. When he was not working with Tyndareus on their plans for a campaign to retake Mycenae, he would hang about watching her work at her loom, or stalk her at a distance when she walked alone in the palace gardens, thinking her own thoughts. His attentions were all the more infuriating in that he could never bring himself to say anything. He would only blush and look miserable when she dismissed him with some cruel remark or other and, as she said to him one day, she would rather be shut up for ever in some gloomy castle than have to endure his hangdog face following her about like a shade. So, despising her father, resentful of her sister, furious at her mother's defection, and disdainful of the company round her, Clytaemnestra wanted nothing more than to get away from Sparta and live life on her own terms.

And then, two years later, when Helen was still only twelve years old, something happened which altered the life of the girls for ever. In northern Thessaly, far across the Isthmus from Sparta, the wife of King Pirithous the Lapith had died. When his time of mourning was over, Pirithous took ship to visit his old friend Theseus of Athens, who had fallen in a bad way when his wife Phaedra hanged herself after owning the blame for the death of his son Hippolytos. Pirithous was looking to lift Theseus's spirits, for these two ageing heroes had fought side by side many times, both as kings and pirates, and always brought out the dare-devil in each other. It wasn't long before they fell to talking about Helen's fabled beauty. The wine did its work. Both men were restless for excitement. Pirithous set about persuading Theseus that they should mount an expedition to kidnap so desirable a prize. They knew that Tyndareus was away from Sparta, leading his army in a bloody campaign to restore his young ally Agamemnon to the Mycenaean throne. Sparta's defences would be weak with no more than a rearguard keeping watch. It was a perfect opportunity. If the snatch was successful, Pirithous suggested, they could draw lots afterwards to see which of them should keep the girl.

Nevertheless it was a risky enterprise, and one made riskier by a sacrilegious act. When they advanced their small band of adventurers through the passes into the Laconian plain, they came across Helen in a woodland shrine where she was offering a sacrifice to Artemis with her friends. The chance was too good to miss. Pirithous grabbed the screaming girl and threw her over his saddle-bow. The kidnappers rode out of the sacred precinct, leaving her friends shouting and wailing behind them.

Once they had shaken off their pursuers, they drew lots as agreed, and Helen fell to Theseus.

Theseus was then more than forty years older than his captive. There had been a time when he would no more have dreamed of harming such a girl than he would have dreamed of ravishing his own child, and it seems that not every trace of his noble soul had quite expired. Perhaps he recalled the hero he had once been when he lived with Hippolyta the Amazon and they fought side by side in defence of Athens against the invading Scythians. Perhaps his conscience was stung by the memory of some insult that Phaedra might have given him. Or perhaps the curse of Virgin Artemis was on him. Whatever the case, some glimmer of sense must have returned to the old man's mind, for as he gazed into the frightened eyes of the young girl lying naked beneath him, he found it impossible to take her.

After a time, miserable and ashamed, he pulled away.

Instantly Helen closed her slender arms across her breast, drew up her legs, and lay trembling like the terrified child she was. Theseus sat for a while shaking his head, appalled that he had sunk so low. 'It's all right,' he was muttering. 'I won't hurt you. It's all right. It's all right.' He could hear the small, panting sobs of her breath. He saw that she was shivering. When he leaned over to cover her body with his cloak, he almost swooned with shame at the sight of such innocent beauty petrified with fear. He tried to comfort the girl but she would not be comforted. So he looked down on her sadly, saying, 'To be gifted with such beauty must be less a blessing than a curse.' And though he had been speaking to himself the words were blazed forever on Helen's mind.

Unable to return her to Sparta, and knowing that he could no longer keep her with him, Theseus entrusted Helen to the charge of one of his more reliable barons at Aphidna in Attica, and sent his own mother Aethra to care for her. Then he took to wandering again until he fetched up at last at the court of King Lycomedes on the island of Skyros. It was there that he died shortly afterwards, having fallen – or leapt – from a windy cliff that overlooks the sea.

Shortly after Helen's abduction, and before news of it had reached him, Sparta was visited by Tantalus, the young King of Elis. Having recently come to his throne, he was looking for a wife and had heard of Helen's beauty. But on his arrival in Sparta he found the city in a state of chaos with the king away at war and his favourite daughter ravished into captivity. As befitted his royal status, Tantalus was lodged in an apartment of the palace and it was there, in one of the state rooms, that he came upon Clytaemnestra.

By now she was approaching marriageable age and had developed a dark, strong-boned glamour of her own. When Tantalus sought to console her for the loss of her sister, he was amazed to discover that this intense young woman was in a frenzy of guilt because she had been praying secretly that Helen would never return. He encouraged her to talk and felt his sympathies stirred. When he remembered that he too had come to Sparta in search of Helen without sparing so much as a thought for her sister, his feelings deepened. They talked of other matters. Again he was surprised by the range of this young woman's interests and the quality of her mind. And as she relaxed, he was entertained too by her witty comments on her own predicament and the weaknesses of those around her. Soon he was in love.

Tantalus talked to Clytaemnestra about his kingdom. It lay beyond Arcadia beside the western sea, two hundred miles to the north, far away from Sparta. Zeus was worshipped there as first among the gods, and a lively festival of games was held in the Sky-Father's honour on the plain at Olympia. His own city of Pisa lay close by that sanctuary, and though it was not so large as Sparta, it was cultured and prosperous, and lacked for nothing but a queen. If Clytaemnestra would give him her consent, he would send messengers to her father asking if his elder daughter might be allowed to grace the throne of Elis.

Clytaemnestra was thinking very quickly. She was under no illusions about Tantalus. He was neither the wealthiest nor the most handsome king in Argos. He had a homely face, with a somewhat pointy nose and ears that stood a little too eagerly to attention. But he was a man of feeling, and gifted with a generous disposition. He was royal and came of an ancient house, yet he had interesting thoughts on how a state might be ruled for the welfare of its subjects without recourse to despotic power. Also he had plans to renovate his city and furnish it with all that was best in modern culture. And he was intelligent. She felt that she might talk to him about absolutely anything and that he would approach each subject with an open mind. After only an hour or so of conversation she had been impressed by his fine discriminating intellect and a range of cultural reference that left her feeling less educated than she had thought – though not humiliatingly so. Tantalus was far too kind for that.

All of this was a great deal, but more important than any of those considerations was the simple fact that he wanted *her*. He wanted her and not her sister. Since he had first learned of her plight and expressed a sincere anxiety for her well-being, Helen's name had scarcely crossed his lips. He seemed as surprised by this fact as she was herself, but Clytaemnestra saw all the greater earnest of his honesty in that.

And with a little effort and imagination, his kingdom could be heavenly.

Was it possible that the gods had begun to smile on her blighted life at last? She could make a new life with this man, a good life, the kind of life that she had always wanted, a life where she could put her own fine mind to use and do rather more than raise babies and wait for her husband to come home from the wars with a sulky gaggle of concubines in tow.

Yet she also knew that if Tantalus spoke to her father now there could be only one reply.

At a time when Tyndareus had his hands full with the struggle for Mycenae, his favourite daughter had been stolen from him. Helen had vanished into thin air somewhere between Sparta and Athens, and her father would think of nothing else till he had found her, brought her back home, and finished the business that would leave Mycenae in grateful vassalage to Sparta.

At such a time, when there was, in fact, no certainty that Helen would ever return, Tyndareus would have no interest in marrying his elder daughter off to a minor monarch with comparatively little wealth and less power, who lived somewhere west of everywhere important. He would say no. He would say it very loudly, and not least, Clytaemnestra suspected, because her father secretly entertained hopes of sealing a new Mycenaean alliance by giving her in marriage to Agamemnon.

That was a thing she would never permit to happen.

For a moment, therefore, she contemplated elopement. But she saw at once that such a course would be disastrous. If Tyndareus came home to find that, with one daughter taken from him, the other had defected of her own free will, his anger would be terrible. Battle-hardened Spartan troops would soon come marching into Elis. Tantalus would not live long enough to argue his case. She would be dragged back home a widow. Clytaemnestra could see the pictures in her mind and could have wept at them.

She shared both her hopes and her fears with Tantalus. They discussed the difficulties, and though he declared himself ready to fight for her, she knew her father's temper and strength better than he did. She saw that haste on their part could put everything at risk, so it would be necessary for them to wait. She was not yet quite of marriageable age but would soon be so. If she swore on her maiden honour that she would never agree to wed any other man, would Tantalus wait for her? Once Tyndareus was back from the war and Helen was rescued, he would be in a more tractable mood. Clytaemnestra would make it plain to him that she would marry Tantalus or no one. And she was prepared to make her father's life a misery until he agreed to what she wanted. In two years, three at the most, she would have won his consent. And then they would be free to live as they wished with nothing to fear from anyone. Was this not the wise thing to do?

They agreed that it was. Tantalus returned to Elis. In a restless dream of longing, Clytaemnestra waited.

Over a year had passed before the spies despatched by Tyndareus across Argos learned where Helen was being held. He sent a force to rescue her and the stronghold at Aphidna fell before it. Theseus's mother Aethra was taken into slavery, and Helen was brought back to Sparta in triumph.

As the war for Mycenae approached its conclusion, Tyndareus was still away at the front, but Clytaemnestra was appalled by the change in her sister. A girl who had once been adventurous and bold had turned into a nervous creature who lived inside her beauty like a woman trapped inside a fearful dream. She had been kept locked away in the draughty citadel at Aphidna, beyond public gaze, with only Aethra and her serving-women for company. And though she had seen nothing more of Theseus and Pirithous, she was still haunted by memories of her abduction – the smell of horse-sweat and saddle-leather as the raiders galloped off with her, the numb terror of watching two old men throwing dice as she trembled between them, the weight of Theseus's body pressing her down.

And the words he had spoken still rang in her ears. Her beauty was a curse, his judgement on it was a curse, and it seemed to Helen now that her whole life was cursed. She was afraid of the world around her. Beyond the confines of the palace, even Sparta, her homeland woods and hills that she had once wandered freely as a deer, had turned into places filled with dark imaginings. She became afraid of the avid way men looked at her whenever she stepped outside the women's quarters, as though every passing glance seemed to threaten a wishful act of rape. Her eyes, which had always possessed the power to leave men standing breathless, took on a hunted look. She felt safe only in the company of Aethra, who had, strangely, become a kind of mother to her during her time of captivity. So Helen chose to remain secluded at her side, scarcely speaking, avoiding the light.

Only gradually did the extent of her sister's fears become clear to Clytaemnestra, and the more her understanding grew the more her anxiety increased. She tried to persuade Helen that her fears were groundless, affording her all the gentle attention she could give. Whatever resentment there might have been between them, they were sisters after all, and she had a duty of care as well as a horrified, sympathetic awareness of how helpless all women were when men took it into their heads to behave in a way that would shame the beasts. But when she tried to encourage Helen to venture out into the world with her again, Clytaemnestra met only with panic-stricken refusals that she took for a kind of self-defeating obstinacy, and she lost patience when all her efforts seemed to make no difference. Beginning to dread that when their father returned he would expect her to carry on caring for her sister until she was well again or until she could be suitably married off, Clytaemnestra told herself that she had a life of her own to live, away from Helen, away from Sparta. It was a life for which she was increasingly impatient.

Then word came that the war was won at Mycenae. The usurper Thyestes was dead. Agamemnon had ascended to his throne. Tyndareus would soon come home. He rejoiced at the thought of seeing his beloved Helen again, and he had news that would excite Clytaemnestra's heart.

The decision to flee Sparta before her father's return was hastily taken but never for a moment regretted, for the year and a half that Clytaemnestra spent as the wife of King Tantalus in Elis proved to be the only unquestionably happy time in her life.

They were fortunate to be allowed so long. Their life together would have been ended sooner but for a development of which Clytaemnestra was ignorant when she fled. When he had first heard the news of Helen's abduction, the shock knocked Tyndareus off his feet as though he had been struck down by a god. For a time after he came round, his behaviour was so vague and uncertain that his friends feared that he had lost his wits. He also complained of numbness in his leg when he walked, so he had been forced to take things easy for a time, entrusting the campaign to Agamemnon's leadership. Tyndareus steamed and fumed like a hot spring in the tent where he lay, until eventually, by sheer strength of will, he got back on his feet again and returned to the battle. But things had changed in his absence. Even his own

Spartan warriors looked to the vigorous young leadership of Agamemnon now. He was the future, and that old warhorse Tyndareus was the past. Once Mycenae was regained, men had no doubt where the ruling power in Argos would lie.

Tyndareus saw that he needed the marriage between Agamemnon and his daughter more than ever, and not merely as an act of patronage to a younger ally, but as the only sure means of maintaining the security of Sparta. He could only thank the gods that, for reasons best known to himself, the elder son of Atreus favoured Clytaemnestra over Helen, whose whereabouts were still unknown.

Then the gods smiled on him again. Helen was found and rescued. After Aphidna was taken, Menestheus, who had succeeded Theseus as king in Athens, hastened to dissociate himself from his predecessor's crime. And in the following weeks the power of Thyestes began to crumble at last. The gate into Mycenae was sold, Thyestes fled the city and was cut down. Regrettably, his son Aegisthus – the murderer of Atreus – contrived to escape, but no one doubted that a great victory had been won, and one that signalled an even more momentous change in the times.

Tyndareus was already on his way home when he was told that Clytaemnestra had eloped to the city of Pisa in Elis where she was to marry King Tantalus. He erupted into rage so violent that the god struck him down again, and he entered Sparta less as a conquering hero than as an ageing cripple with trembling hands and slurred speech.

He was certainly in no shape to lead an army into Elis. Nor could he count on Agamemnon for immediate help because the young Lion of Mycenae would have his hands full for some time, securing his power base in the city, taking charge of its finances and administration and asserting his authority over the outlying domains. So Clytaemnestra and her husband were left in peace for many months, though the temper of the messages reaching them from Sparta left Tantalus in no doubt that he had better prepare for war.

War came shortly after the birth of their first child. By that time Agamemnon was ready to expand his empire and there were urgent reasons why he was drawn first to Elis. When he marched into that country at the head of his troops, Tantalus decided to meet him in the field rather than allowing him to lay siege to Pisa. He chose his ground well, intercepting the invaders at a narrow pass through the mountains where he commanded the heights.

But Agamemnon had learned a great deal through the way Mycenae had finally fallen to treachery. Tantalus ordered his army to charge and drove his chariot down towards the Mycenaean line. Only when he was too far advanced to turn back did he realize how few of his warriors had followed. The rest, convinced that sooner or later Elis must fall to the overwhelming might of Mycenae, had been bought off and were now Agamemnon's men.

Clytaemnestra learned of her husband's defeat as the Mycenaeans marched into the palace at Pisa. Terrified and distraught, she was clutching her infant son to her breast when Agamemnon burst open the chamber door. He snatched the child from her, gave it to one of his men with orders to bash out its brains, and informed Clytaemnestra that she was now a widow and would shortly be remarried.

Only with difficulty was she restrained from killing herself. Then, for a time, she fought him off like a lynx. But this strange, grim man, who had been obsessed by her for many years, doggedly laid siege to her.

When Clytaemnestra demanded in outrage how he could imagine that she would ever give herself to the murderer of her child, he told her that if he had spared the child, it would only have grown up looking to avenge its father – such was the way of things in the bloody history of Mycenae. Nor, he pointed out, was she the first woman to have been seized as a prize in war, and unlike most of the rest she was not condemned to the life of a concubine or a slave.

On the contrary, she was about to be married to a man who

had loved her like a faithful hound for years, and would become the wealthiest wife in all Argos. For if the gods had gifted the house of Aeacus with power, and the house of Amythaon with wisdom, they had blessed the house of Atreus with wealth. And where there was wealth there was power, and that surely, Agamemnon declared, was wisdom enough for any woman in her right mind.

So he left her alone to think things over for a time. Then one night he came to her with wine and gifts. He was trying to make a suitor of himself, and with every awkward gesture she could feel her hatred for him coursing through her veins. But there was a moment when she saw among the bluff crags of his face the eyes of the frightened boy who, many years before, had fled with his brother out of the bloody butcher's cave that was Mycenae. In that moment she sensed the power she might wield through him and over him.

Later, much later, he mounted her like a bull, and she let him take what was neither of meaning nor of value to her now. But her spirit – she vowed it as she lay with her eyes open – would remain for ever, and inalienably, her own.

In the meantime, Helen had found new purpose in her life by caring for her father. Tyndareus had always been soft with his younger daughter and pliant to her will. Even though he had been party to her sister's terrible suffering, he knew that Helen would never enquire into his actions too closely, and was grateful now to consign his weakened body to her care. So with Aethra in constant attendance, and her lovelorn cousin Penelope for company, Helen would have been content to live this quiet life indefinitely. But the world still had demands to make on her.

As Agamemnon brought Elis under subjugation and kingdom after kingdom acknowledged the supremacy of Mycenae, a time of peace settled across Argos. Young men whose thoughts had largely been given over to war began to think of marriage, and Helen – who was reputed to be the most beautiful woman ever to grace the earth – was now of marriageable age. Whoever was lucky enough to marry her would also shortly succeed to the throne of Sparta. So Helen soon became the unrivalled object of desire for all the great princes of Argos.

One by one they presented themselves as suitors at the court of Tyndareus, each of them bearing rich gifts and strutting in their finery like courting birds, or making an impressive show, like bull-seals, of their strength and prowess.

Among those most infatuated by Helen's beauty was Diomedes, Lord of Tiryns, who was renowned as one of the bravest of men. Unaware of her nervous temperament, or perhaps insensitive to it, he sought to impress her with stories of his triumph in the long and terrible war at Thebes. Helen listened to him patiently and gave him small signs of her favour, but withheld any certain answer to his eager proposal of marriage.

Menestheus of Athens was less warmly received. Though he was at pains to distinguish himself from his predecessor Theseus, he brought back memories of her confinement in Attica and was too evidently self-seeking in his manner. He would have been sent away with a clear rejection had Tyndareus not advised his daughter to reject no one yet for fear of stirring hostility to Sparta. So Idomeneus, heir to the Cretan King Deucalion, sailed from Knossos to plead his suit, and out of Salamis came Ajax, the valiant son of Telamon, along with his step-brother Teucer, who had been fathered on Telamon's captive bride Hesione. The great archer Philoctetes came from Aeolia, bringing the massive bow that Heracles had bequeathed to him in return for his armour-bearer's willingness to light his funeral pyre on Mount Oeta, and many others made the journey by land across the Peloponnese.

All together, there were thirty-eight contenders for Helen's hand, most of them mature warriors, men of power and influence who had already made their reputations. But among them were two young men of much the same age as Helen herself. Not yet seventeen, Palamedes, the Prince of Euboea, proved far more intelligent than any of his rivals, whom he kept amused by teaching them a complicated new game he had invented. The movement of stones across a patterned board according to the throw of dice provided a volatile form of gambling, from which Palamedes seemed to profit with astonishing regularity. The other young man had much less to say for himself but he carried his diffident good looks with a proud reserve and a strong, noble bearing. It was generally agreed that he stood little chance, but this graduate of Cheiron's school impressed everyone by the courteous modesty of his demeanour. His name was Patroclus, son of Menoetius.

Helen sat at the centre of all this attention in a state of panic. She had seen what had happened to her sister, who had now provided Agamemnon with an heir yet seemed to have surrendered all hope of happiness in this life. She watched as her uncle Icarius refused to allow his daughter Penelope to marry the man with whom she was clearly in love. And she had long since begun to wonder whether her own life could ever be anything more than a trophy to be grabbed by the strongest contender. Yet she also saw that her father could not have much longer to live, and that the world would give her no peace until she belonged to some other man. Sooner or later a choice must be made among the gang of suitors clamouring for her attention.

Tyndareus would also have preferred to despatch the contenders and carry on living a quiet life at the centre of his daughter's world. With so many mighty princes vying for Helen's hand, and feelings running high, he was uncertain how to favour any one of them without incurring the enmity of the others. And the risk of such enmity was increased by the fact that, of all the candidates, one had stronger claims on him than all the rest, and could exert more pressure.

Menelaus, the younger son of Atreus, had loved Helen with a passion for many years, and Tyndareus could see that Helen found a familiar gentleness and consideration in Agamemnon's milder brother that was less threatening to her than the claims of strangers.

Since the days of his boyhood, she had always responded with loving friendship to the shy, slightly askance smile with which he faced the world, as though it had always come at him like a big wind. But Menelaus was no longer a boy. He was a seasoned warrior who bore the mark of the wars in a scar that ran down his right cheek and clipped the corner of his mouth, fixing it in a wry tuck of the skin. And if he lacked his brother's oppressive bluster, he remained nevertheless a son of Atreus. Should he become King of Sparta through marriage to Helen, the brothers would have effective control of the entire Peloponnesus. Some of the others contending for Helen's hand, and the power that went with it, might be sufficiently worried by such a prospect to take steps to prevent it.

So Tyndareus dithered, and Helen was content to let him do so.

Fortunately, among that rowdy gathering of gallants Tyndareus had one resourceful friend. Odysseus, Prince of Ithaca, had come to Sparta not in the hope of snatching Helen from under the noses of much richer men, but to pursue a different claim of his own. Tyndareus had a brother called Icarius and he too had a desirable daughter. If less astonishingly beautiful than her cousin, Penelope had a poise and dignity that enchanted the heart of the Ithacan, and a shrewd intelligence that delighted his agile mind. But her father Icarius — a stiff-necked man who liked to assert what little power he had — was looking for a more prosperous son-in-law than the relatively penurious prince of a small island in the Ionian sea, and he made it plain from the first that he neither liked nor trusted this adventurer out of Ithaca.

His daughter might pine as long as she liked, he insisted, but sooner or later she would see the good sense of his opposition. Why on earth would she want to wear herself out in a hand-to-mouth life with a man who was no better than a pirate on a barren rock somewhere to the west of civilization, when she could take her pick among any of the princes that her more obedient cousin refused?

Penelope had only a single reason – a reason which satisfied her as much as it exasperated Icarius: she loved Odysseus and was more than happy to spend the rest of her life with him, however hard that life might be. So to her father's angry frustration, she remained obstinate in her resolve to marry no one else. But her nature was also too modest and loyal to do what her lover urged and compromise her reputation by an impetuous elopement.

Caught between two stubborn, Spartan temperaments, Odysseus eventually came to Tyndareus with his problem.

'We both seem to find ourselves in difficulties,' he said. 'I wonder if we can't be of assistance to one another.'

Tyndareus sighed. Knowing Odysseus of old, he had guessed that this scrawny fellow with short legs, bristling hair and a knocked-askew nose was fishing for something from the moment he'd requested this private audience. But his guest's rascally smile made a welcome change from the laconic gravity of those around him, and he could at least relax in the knowledge that the Ithacan was not in contention for his daughter's hand.

'Explain,' he said, and signalled for his cup-bearer to pour more wine.

Odysseus took the measure of the man across from him – a man well past his prime, more than twice his own age, who had once been a formidable warrior and was now reduced to the condition of a pampered cripple. Deciding that a breezy impudence might serve his purpose best, he said, 'It seems clear to me which way the wind blows.'

Tyndareus tilted his head.

'I've been watching Agamemnon lean his weight on you. The Mycenean lion is pushing his brother's cause, of course, but he also wants this marriage to consolidate the alliance between Sparta and the house of Atreus.' Odysseus glanced sharply up at the old Spartan king. 'My guess is that he has ambitions abroad, and with Sparta safely in his brother's hands, his power would be secured at home.'

In the slurred speech that was all he could manage these days,

Tyndareus whispered, 'The throne of Sparta is already occupied.'

'And by the wisest of kings,' Odysseus smiled. 'But you won't live for ever, old friend. And whoever marries Helen warms his bed with a woman as close to a goddess as a man can hope to get and inherits your kingdom.'

Tyndareus reproved his manner with a weary sigh. 'Your point?'

'My point is, I think it's what you want too. Marry Helen to Menelaus, make him your heir, and Sparta becomes unshakeable.' Odysseus grinned across at the old king, whose trembling hand fidgeted with a serpent arm-ring twisted round his wrist. 'Add to this the convenient fact that Menelaus seems to be sincerely insane with love for your daughter, and Helen knows that he'll take good care of her, then the marriage makes sense in every way.'

'Do you think that none of this has occurred to me?'

'But it's not quite so simple, is it? Disappoint any of the other ambitious princes here and you could have a deal of trouble on your hands.'

Tyndareus glanced away.

Odysseus brought his hands together at his lips. 'I think I can see a solution.' He smiled. 'But it comes at a price.'

Tyndareus turned to look at him again, narrow-eyed. 'Save your breath,' he said. 'My brother's face is set against you.'

Odysseus opened his palms. 'The King sees through me. But there are things he might say to his brother which I cannot say myself. He might tell him, for instance, that Odysseus of Ithaca has recently pulled off a number of successful ventures and is far richer than when he was last in Sparta.'

'Piracy will not endear you to him!'

Again Odysseus smiled. 'But a glance into my coffers might. And could he name me a royal house that was not founded on brigandage or piracy?'

Tyndareus grunted. 'How much richer?'

'Enough to make a couple of Lycian towns and several Sidonian merchants considerably poorer. Icarius will have his bride-price, and he can rest assured that his daughter will want for nothing when she comes to Ithaca.'

Tyndareus shook his head. 'Icarius looks to have her as Queen in Crete.'

Odysseus shook his head. 'There is bad blood in the House of the Axe. Penelope will not give herself to Deucalion's son.'

'Temper your speech,' Tyndareus frowned. 'The Cretan is my houseguest.'

'As is the better part of Argive royalty – eating your food and emptying your wine-cellar while you and your brother dither over your daughters' futures.'

Odysseus sighed impatiently now. 'Penelope wants only me for her husband. She wants me as certainly as Helen wants Menelaus, and if you and Icarius wish to sleep easier in your beds at night you would both do well to let your daughters have their way.'

But Tyndareus merely scowled. 'This is all the solution you have? I had expected something more ingenious.'

'That is part of it,' said Odysseus, smiling again, 'but not the whole. The rest I keep to myself till you agree to plead my cause with Icarius.'

Tyndareus studied the irrepressible sea-rover across from him. He guessed that Odysseus had already been in conference with Menelaus and Agamemnon and that they knew what he was about right now. He guessed that he'd discussed this business with Helen too, and that all three had felt what he was feeling: that something about this guileful rogue inspired one's confidence, even if you weren't quite sure you could trust him.

'What do you want me to say,' he sighed.

'It's simple enough,' Odysseus answered. 'Tell him that you've been thinking things over and that you've decided that the only sensible thing for a father to do in such a pass is to leave his daughter free to choose for herself. Tell him that's what you will let Helen do, and that if he cares for his own daughter's happiness, he should do the same for Penelope. Tell him Odysseus has been at pains to mend his fortune for his daughter's sake, and that not only does he love Penelope with undying passion, he's also a far more resourceful and reliable fellow than the scoundrel that Icarius mistakes him for. Tell him what you know to be true – that Penelope loves me and will continue to make his life a misery until he consents to this marriage.'

'And if I agree,' said Tyndareus, hearing nothing there that would come hard to his lips, 'shall I tell him that the resourceful Odysseus has helped me find a way out of my difficulties?'

'You shall.'

'And that way is?'

'Do we have a bargain?' Odysseus held out his hand. When Tyndareus nodded and took it, the Ithacan smiled. 'Tomorrow is the day when the King Horse must be sacrificed to Poseidon, is it not?'

'What of it?'

'Here is what you must do. Assemble all the suitors in the sacred precinct and tell them that with so many proud princes to choose among, you have been unable to see any other way than to leave Helen free to make the decision for herself. Tell them that is how it will be. But also tell them that before her choice is announced you will require every man present to swear a vow that he will defend her chosen husband against anyone who challenges his right to have her.'

Tyndareus sat back in his chair, stroking his beard. After a moment he said, 'Men have been known to break their oaths.'

Again Odysseus grinned. 'I have an oath in mind so terrible,' he said, 'that not one of them will dare to break it.'

The King Horse was brought in from his pasture at dawn the next day. With his mane and tail braided and garlanded, and his hooves painted gold, the sleek white stallion was led into the sacred precinct where the bronze statue of Poseidon brandished his trident fish-spear. There the stallion was offered to the god before all the assembled suitors. But the great beast did not go easily to the sacrifice. It was as if his nostrils already smelled death coming to him. He snorted and whinnied with rolling eyes. His ears were laid back and hooves restive as Tyndareus invoked the blue-haired god who moves both earth and sea. It took four men straining with all their weight against his rawhide tethers to keep the powerful animal in place.

The old king lacked the strength to ensure a clean kill, so it was his son-in-law, Agamemnon, acting as his surrogate, who took the sacred cleaver in hand and smote the sinews of the horse's neck, severing the windpipe with a single blow. Wide-eyed, screaming his grief and rage, the King Horse reared back against the tethers, flailing bright hooves against the air. He seemed to hang there for a long time as though gathering the force to trample death beneath him, then he frothed out his last gasps of breath before collapsing in his death throes at Agamemnon's feet. Blood spurted from the torn white flesh into a silver salver. Steam rose in the morning heat, and as flies began to gather, the men who had restrained the horse took cleavers of their own and began to joint the carcass till the once majestic animal lay in raw and bloody pieces on the precinct's holy ground.

Only then did Tyndareus announce to the suitors the terms of the oath that Odysseus had devised for them. Before his daughter declared the name of he who was to be the happy recipient of her hand, each of these mighty princes was required to stand with one foot on a portion of the great white stallion that had been offered to Poseidon, and ask that the god should visit ruin and destruction on his lands if he failed to defend the right of the successful candidate to hold Helen alone and unchallenged for the rest of his days.

For a few moments while they took in the gravity of what was being asked of them, the assembled princes stood in silence. A stir and murmur passed through the throng as they recalled the terrible havoc that had been wrought in living memory by angry shrugs of the Earthshaker's shoulders in Knossos and in Troy. Tyndareus glanced uncertainly at Odysseus, who merely smiled and gave a reassuring nod. 'Come, gentlemen,' said

Agamemnon, 'is not so dreadful an oath warranted by so fair a prize?'

Young Palamedes spoke up first. 'I for one will gladly make this pledge – though I confess I would rather have played dice for Helen's hand!' An uneasy laugh rippled among the suitors. Then Palamedes said, 'But should not he who devised so dreadful an oath be the first to utter it?'

Unprepared for this, Odysseus took in the general murmur of agreement. 'All men know that I am not a contender here,' he prevaricated.

'No more am I,' said Agamemnon, eager to move things on, 'but I too will gladly swear. Come, Lord Odysseus, show us how the thing is done.'

So Odysseus found himself with no choice but to untie his sandal and stand with his bare foot pressed against a portion of the horse's thigh to put his honour and the fate of his island at the mercy of Earthshaker Poseidon.

Agamemnon was next to take the oath. Then Diomedes, eager to display his love for Helen, stepped forward. Menelaus, Palamedes and the handsome Prince of Crete were quick to join them. One by one, with fear of the god heavy on their tongues, the others followed. Only when all the princes had sworn did Helen step forth in her bridal gown, holding the wreath she had made for this sacred occasion, and place it over the flowing red hair of Menelaus, who stood, beaming with joy, among the rivals he had bested.

'The gods are just,' he cried, with tears starting at his eyes. 'My thanks go forth to Divine Athena for guiding the choice of my betrothed.' Then looking at the number and quality of the men around him, and the glower of envy and disappointment in their eyes, he turned to the statue of the god. 'Hear my praises, Great Poseidon, Ruler of Horses and Shaker of Cities, for granting your divine protection to this union.'

Helen told herself again that Menelaus had always been her friend. Now he would be her safe haven in the turmoil of the world, and if, as a girl, she had ever dreamed of passion, she was glad to let go of such dreams. She wanted to believe that when she gave her body to Menelaus that night, the act would allay the curse of her beauty for ever. She wanted to believe it with all her heart. But the heart is a prophetic organ and can, for a time, keep secrets even from the one inside whose breast it beats.

Meanwhile, Tyndareus opened his arms to give the younger son of Atreus his blessing. He watched Agamemnon and Clytaemnestra gather Menelaus and Helen into their embrace, brother to brother and sister to sister. And as he did so, the weary old king was reflecting on the day many years earlier when, in sacrificing to the gods, he had foolishly neglected to make an offering to Aphrodite, and the Golden One had sworn to take her revenge by making sure that both his daughters would one day prove to be faithless wives.

The Supplicant

Within the year Tyndareus was found dead in his chamber. Already ruler in all but name, Menelaus ascended to the Lacadaemonian throne of Sparta, and shortly afterwards his beloved wife gave birth to a daughter. Helen's labour was so long and hard that there was a time when Aethra feared that the struggle might kill her, yet the infant Hermione emerged from those birth-pangs with so much of her mother's exquisite beauty that Menelaus felt more than ever blessed in the marriage he had made.

Helen too was strengthened by the marriage. With the long ordeal of being the object of every man's desire now over, her confidence returned. She took a new purchase on life, responding well to the pleasures and challenges of being a wife, a mother and a queen. In dealing with the affairs of a kingdom whose customs she knew and understood far better than he did, Menelaus often sought her counsel. This was the first time that anyone had ever valued her judgement, and she thrived on it, discovering a larger interest in public life. They drew up new plans for their palace together, extending both the state rooms and their private apartments, and making skilful use at her suggestion of the finely mottled porphyry from local quarries. The results so impressed her sister that Clytaemnestra ordered large quantities of Spartan stone for the refurbishment of her own gloomy palace in Mycenae.

Helen also took delight in redesigning the gardens around their home so that the tranquil hours that she and her adoring husband spent together with their child might be filled with fragrance and colour and the sound of water.

At such times they could look down from their palace beneath the Bronze House of Athena across a broad fertile plain ringed by its steep defending hills, on to a future in which their contentment seemed assured. For if there was little passion in their life together there was a great deal of affection, and Sparta was prospering around them. Already plans were laid for the day when Hermione would marry her cousin Orestes, the first-born child of Agamemnon and Clytaemnestra, thus uniting the thrones of Sparta and Mycenae for ever. The gods, it seemed, were kind.

Almost four years after the birth of Hermione, Menelaus received an urgent message from his brother. Agamemnon required his presence at the court of King Telamon on Salamis, where their joint show of strength would offer support to the king in the latest round of a long-standing wrangle with Troy.

Dismayed by the prospect of this first separation from her husband, Helen demanded to know why such a mission should be necessary.

'It's an old quarrel,' Menelaus explained. 'Telamon and Heracles captured Troy about thirty years ago and as part of his share in the spoils Telamon was given the Trojan King's daughter Hesione. She's been kept on Salamis against her will ever since and wants nothing more than to go home. When Priam first succeeded to his father's throne he was too weak to help his sister. These days he's one of the most powerful kings in the east, and he's determined to release her, but Telamon has turned down every offer of ransom.'

Firmly Helen said, 'I was once held captive in a strange land and I know the pain of it. If Hesione is miserable on Salamis, Telamon should let her go.'

Menelaus grunted and looked away.

'Why won't he?' she demanded.

'Because he's a hot-headed old war-horse who thinks he's the last of the heroes since Heracles and Theseus died. Sometimes I think he'd watch Salamis burn sooner than give up his rightful prize.'

'But that's just foolishness,' Helen protested. 'And anyway, I don't see how any of this concerns Sparta.'

'Telamon has asked for Agamemnon's support. Agamemnon has asked for mine. He's my brother. I have to go.'

He spoke as if that should be the end of the matter but Helen refused to be deterred. 'Don't you agree that it would be for the best if Hesione was given her wish and returned to her home in Troy?'

'Of course I do.' Menelaus frowned. 'But we can't just let the Trojans take her or they'll begin to think that Argos is weak.'

She said, 'That sounds more like your brother than yourself.'

He gave her a reassuring smile that puckered the scar at his lip. 'But I'm not my brother, and that's why it's important that I go to Salamis. It should be possible to sort this quarrel out without violence, and I think I might be able to act as a moderating influence.'

Uncertainly Helen nodded, hoping that he was right.

Meanwhile in Troy, King Priam had become so exasperated by Telamon's rejection of his many generous offers to ransom Hesione that he was ready to threaten war over the issue. His counsellor Antenor, firm in his conviction that Troy's interests were best served by peace, was opposed to such a dangerous course and called for support in his caution from Priam's cousin Anchises, the blind King of the Dardanians. Anchises reminded Priam of the disaster that had ensued the last time Troy came into conflict with the Argives. And since Agamemnon had been declared High King, those warlike tribes were no longer fighting each other. If Priam invaded Salamis, all Argos might come down about his ears.

Though he listened impatiently, Priam could hear the sense of it and reluctantly agreed that it would be wise not to resort to arms until all hope of a diplomatic solution was exhausted. So Anchises and Antenor were sent as his ambassadors to Salamis with a fresh, and final, demand for Hesione's return.

Menelaus arrived on the island two days after the Trojan legation and found his brother Agamemnon already there. Fortified by the presence of allies, Telamon, who was now well into his fifties and had put on a great deal of weight, called a council at which he invited Anchises and Antenor to state their case. Having heard them without interest, he turned to Agamemnon with a dismissive gesture. 'Every year I must listen to such wheedling and bluster. Since they got fat and rich the Trojans have turned into moaning old women – though I don't recall hearing Priam complain when – out of a generosity of spirit I've since come to regret – I allowed Hesione to ransom his life. Don't you agree it's time this nonsense was settled once and for all?'

Agamemnon nodded, 'Hesione was justly taken. Laomedon broke his word – as Troy has been prone to do. His perfidy cost him his city and all its spoils. There can be no question but that the woman is rightfully yours.'

Telamon's sons agreed. Menelaus said nothing until Agamemnon glanced towards him, when he too nodded, though with less vehement conviction.

Telamon turned to Antenor with a shrug. 'You see. The High King of Argos and his brother the King of Sparta are with me. Go home and tell Priam that both he and his sister would have been dead a long time ago if it wasn't for the merciful gallantry shown to them by myself and Heracles. They should both be thankful rather than testing our patience like this.'

'King Priam's patience also has limits,' said Anchises quietly.

'So a deaf king sends us a blind king as his ambassador!' Telamon glanced at Agamemnon with a mirthless chuckle, and then turned his smirk on the Trojan legation. 'If Priam wants his sister back so badly, he should come and fetch her for himself. Meanwhile I shall use her as I choose.'

'Is there not room for compromise here?' Menelaus put in quickly. 'Perhaps Hesione might be allowed to visit her brother for a time?'

Agamemnon glowered at his brother. Telamon firmly shook his head. 'Let her out of my sight and I'd never see her again. Her place is here with me.'

'And why should Salamis trust the word of Troy when history counsels otherwise?' Agamemnon put in. 'Telamon won Hesione by right of arms. Should he choose to keep her that way, he can rely on our support.'

Shortly afterwards, having suggested that Telamon would be wise to seek more measured counsel than that of the ambitious King of Mycenae, Antenor and Anchises returned gloomily to Troy.

Menelaus also came back from Salamis with a heavy heart, only to find that during his absence pestilence had struck Sparta. Helen had done everything she could to keep the people in good heart, entreating the gods on their behalf and offering help and advice from her wise woman Polydamna. But the first terrible death was followed by another, and soon the contagion began to spread throughout the poorer quarters of the city. Fearful both for his family and for the welfare of his kingdom, Menelaus imposed quarantine around the citadel and sent messengers to the oracle of Apollo at Delphi asking what remedy might be found for the plague that now threatened to ravage his country. After several days the answer came back that the king must seek out the tombs of a wolf and a goat that were brothers, and offer sacrifices there.

For some time the priests and counsellors of the kingdom puzzled over the answer. How could a wolf and a goat possibly be brothers, and why would either be buried in a tomb? At last, after many hours spent poring over the clay tablets in the temple archives, a young scholar-priest emerged with a story to tell. In ancient times, the priest declared, Prometheus, benefactor of men – he who had dared to steal fire from heaven and given to mankind a portion of the qualities possessed by all the other animals – had once fathered two sons on the Harpy Celaeno. The names she gave to them were Lycus and Chimaerus, the wolf and the he-goat. They had been servants of Apollo Smintheus – Apollo of the mice – the god who brought, and who might also cure, pestilence.

'Where are the tombs of these brothers to be found?' demanded Menelaus.

'Across the Aegean Sea,' he was told, 'at Sminthe, in the kingdom of Troy.'

Menelaus threw his hands in the air. 'Sometimes I wonder if the gods are toying with us. This is no good time to be going cap in hand to Troy.'

On the night after the oracle was interpreted, he turned in his bed for so long that Helen too was kept from sleep. 'Shall I ask Polydamna to prepare you a sleeping-draught?' she murmured at last.

'No,' he shook his head and turned again. 'Forgive me for disturbing you. I have much on my mind.'

Gathering a purple shawl about her shoulders, Helen sat up beside her husband and put a hand to his shoulder. 'Tell me,' she said.

'Try to sleep.' He withdrew into his own preoccupations, 'It's enough that one of us should go without rest.'

'Would you rather I nursed my fears in the dark as you do? If something is troubling you, you must share it with me.'

Sighing, Menelaus turned over onto his back. 'The riddle of the oracle was deciphered today. Its judgement is that Sparta can only be freed of pestilence if sacrifices are offered at some ancient tombs near Troy.'

'Then send there at once,' Helen exclaimed. 'Have the offerings made. What is the difficulty?'

Quietly he said, 'I must make the offerings myself.'

'You must voyage to Troy?'

'Yes.'

'Then I will come with you.'

He shook his head, 'No, I want you to stay here and watch over Hermione and the city for me.'

'And what of my wishes? Do they count for nothing? Hermione can come with us,' she added quickly. 'We have counsellors who will care for the city.'

Menelaus sat up to look at his wife. 'I've no more desire to leave you than you have to see me go, my love. But I can't take you with me.'

Sensing that there was more on his mind than he had so far shared, she pushed him further until at last he declared that he was unwilling to take her with him because the journey might well prove dangerous.

'Then we will share the dangers,' she countered. When he shook his head and turned away again, she said, 'What are you not telling me?'

He lay in troubled silence for a time, not wanting to alarm her. But his need to unburden his cares was also great, so when she pressed him again he said, 'I'm afraid that sooner or later war must come between Argos and Troy.'

'Why,' she demanded, 'why should it come to that?'

'Helen, there could be many reasons. Because Priam is an angry old man who has lost patience with Telamon. Because Troy would be the richest of prizes. Because men are fools who think there's more glory to be found in a bloody brawl over a burning city than in cultivating their fields in peace. Perhaps because the gods have grown bored and are spoiling for trouble.'

'Or because your brother is?'

Menelaus glanced away from the cold question. 'All I know is that the air smells of war every time Argives and Trojans jostle each other. It would take no more than a single reckless incident to provide a pretext and the whole eastern seaboard could go up in flames.'

Helen had listened to this with increasing dismay. She sat staring into the darkness now. 'Why have you said nothing of this before?'

'Because I wasn't certain. I didn't want to alarm you.'

'But you're certain now?'

'Not certain, no.' He looked back at her and saw the light from the oil-lamp gleaming in her eyes. 'But you're right of course,' he admitted. 'Since Agamemnon became High King of Argos, it seems as if his hunger for power is feeding on itself. I hadn't quite realized it till I saw him in Salamis but he's been at peace too long and he's looking eastwards now. He's been probing the Asian coast with pirate raids for years, but it's Troy that he wants.'

Helen gave vent to her anger. 'The man's a monster. Is all Argos not enough for him?'

'Apparently not. Fortunately, he can't take Troy on his own and he's not yet certain he can count on all the support he needs. Telamon and his sons would be quick to join him, of course, and there are others who are thinking about the plunder. Diomedes for one. But they wouldn't be enough on their own.'

Helen frowned into the gloom. 'And you?'

Menelaus turned to look at his wife. 'Like it or not, if it came to war I would have to commit the strength of Sparta.'

'Because Agamemnon is right? Or because he's your brother?'

There was a long silence between them.

Eventually Helen said, 'And the oracle demands that you go to Troy at such a time?'

Menelaus sighed. 'The only choice I have is not to take you with me.'

'Then you will go fully armed? You will take ships and fighting-men with you.'

'That would be Agamemnon's way – to go bustling in, demanding access to the tombs and cutting his way through if they so much as blinked at him. But it would start the war I'm trying to avoid. That's why I can't sleep.'

'Then what will you do?'

'I don't know. I just don't know.'

Helen put a hand tenderly to his cheek. 'Then perhaps you should try to sleep on it.' She pushed him gently back down onto the bed and laid her arm across his chest, but neither of them could sleep and they could almost hear each other thinking.

After a time, Helen said, 'What do you think Odysseus would advise if he was here?'

Menelaus thought about it. 'Antenor knows I'm trying to avoid conflict,' he said eventually. 'I'm sure he read it in my face on Salamis. And Anchises isn't looking for war. So I think Odysseus would tell me to go to Troy in a way which meant I could speak easily with them.'

'That sounds wise,' she said, 'but how could it be done?'

'Perhaps only honestly,' he realized quickly. 'Perhaps that's it. I think you've solved it for me. After all, I'm going to Troy as a supplicant so that's how I should present myself – unarmed, a pilgrim on a sacred errand to the god.'

He sat up in bed with sudden excitement. 'I'm sure that's it,' he exclaimed, and took her warmly into his embrace. 'What would I do without you?'

'What will I do without you?' she whispered. 'Are you sure about this?'

'Absolutely sure. And all the more so because the thought came to me through you. And I'll be back in Sparta just as soon as I can. Believe me, a man who shares his bed with the cleverest and most beautiful woman in the world won't stay away a night longer than he needs.'

'But the dangers,' she said.

'The best way of avoiding danger is not to provoke it. I should have seen it for myself. It's going to be all right, I promise you.'

Not long after that Menelaus fell asleep. But Helen lay awake for a long time that night, aware of the darkness behind everything, and fearful that for all her husband's protestations the world was changing round them in ways that neither of them could ever hope to control.

In Troy meanwhile, Priam had again summoned his council. Having listened while Anchises and Antenor reported on the failure of their mission, he said, 'I'm minded to accept Telamon's ungracious invitation. If he refuses our offers of gold then let him have bronze weaponry instead. How soon can we have a fleet ready to invade Salamis?'

'Within a few months,' his eldest son Hector replied, 'but we should think carefully about this. Troy's genius has always been for peace not war. If the High King of Argos should come to Telamon's aid, there may be more to lose here than there is to gain.'

'Hesione has suffered captivity for more than twenty years,' Priam snapped. 'How long would this council have me sit here doing nothing to aid her?'

'I don't doubt my brother's courage,' Deiphobus put in, 'but Hector is too cautious. We Trojans can fight as well as any, and our friends will stand with us. The Argive pirates have troubled our coastline long enough.'

'Mount such an expedition if you think it right,' said Antenor, 'but I greatly fear that war may be all that comes of it. I know the king cares for his sister. He should be aware that Telamon will see her dead sooner than give her up.'

Frowning, Priam looked to his blind cousin. 'Anchises, you were in Salamis. Do you believe that to be so?'

Anchises lifted his head. 'Telamon is a firebrand with an evil temper. Hesione's life means little to him. He's sacked this city once, remember. I could hear in his voice that he thinks he can do it again.'

'Then let him come and try,' said Deiphobus. 'He'll find it a different proposition this time.'

'He's eager to come,' said Antenor, 'and Agamemnon with him. And if Agamemnon comes, then his brother will come, and they will not come alone.'

Priam said heavily, 'When Agamemnon is ready for war he will find all the excuses he needs. The fate of my sister matters nothing to him. He knows that Troy is rich. He knows that we command the Asian seaboard and that we hold the gate to the trade roads of the east. Those are the reasons why he'll bring his ships against us sooner or later.'

'Then if war is coming,' Deiphobus declared, 'we should take it to him before he brings it to us. Let the time be now.'

Less impetuous than his brother, Hector sat at his father's side in the grave silence of the council chamber. After a moment he glanced up at Antenor. 'You said you thought that the younger son of Atreus might have doubts about looking for a war?'

Antenor smiled bleakly. 'The King of Sparta is comfortable enough staying at home in bed with Helen.'

Most of the men in the hall permitted themselves a smile, but Hector was not among them. 'Then might we reason with him?' he asked.

'More easily than with Agamemnon,' said blind Anchises.

'But we can't reason with Telamon,' Priam declared, 'and Menelaus will support his brother if it comes to war. The question is shall it be now or later?'

A new voice said, 'There may be another way.'

Everyone turned to see Paris leaning against a pillar with a half-smile on his lips. It was the first time he had ever spoken in council, but he had been listening eagerly and carefully for many months, while he was taught the rudiments of reading, writing and statecraft. Though the names of Argos and Sparta had been unknown to him when he first heard them at Aphrodite's lips, they were familiar enough to him now, and if, for everyone else, Argos was like the shadow of thunder looming across the prospects of the city, for Paris it was luminous with hope.

Deiphobus said, 'I'm sure our father values your opinion, but we're not discussing the finer points of bull-breeding today.'

'Peace, cousin,' said Aeneas. 'Let the king hear your brother.'

Paris cleared his throat. 'I think my father is wise to build a fleet ready for war. But while it is building, why not let me take ship westwards and see if I can't carry off some Argive princess to hold hostage in exchange for the release of Hesione? Telamon will not listen to us but he may take notice of his angry friends when they demand that he lets her go in return for the woman they have lost. That way we may save my father's sister and still be ready for Agamemnon if he comes against us. And — who knows? — with luck we might even avoid a costly war.'

'Paris is thinking more clearly than the rest of us,' Hector smiled. 'This strikes me as a cunning plan.'

'And one that is rather well-suited to his talents!' Aeneas laughed. 'Once the Argive women set eyes on him, they'll be fighting over which of them gets abducted first. I might even go along myself to watch it happen.'

'Then let it be so,' said Priam gravely and turned to Antenor. 'Have the ship-builder Phereclus summoned. I want a fleet of warships ready for an assault on Salamis before summer's end. My son Paris shall sail in the first of them.'

Two weeks later Paris was down at the shore clad only in a breech-clout as he worked among the shipwrights to help the timbers of his vessel take shape. Beside him Phereclus raised his craftsman's eyes from a further satisfied examination of the figure-head that a wood-carver had delivered earlier that day. 'She can never be as beautiful as the goddess herself,' he was saying, 'but this is as fine an Aphrodite as I've seen in a long time.'

When Paris did not immediately reply, the ship-builder glanced across at him and saw that the young man's attention had been taken elsewhere. A vessel had entered the mouth of the Hellespont and dropped sail while still some way out. Now she was coming in under oars with the sun behind her, leaving the boats of the fishing fleet bobbing in her wake.

Phereclus shielded his eyes to study the approaching vessel. 'She's Argive-built,' he muttered after a moment, 'but no warship. So who do we have here?'

The ship creaked closer inshore and ran aground about thirty yards down the strand. One of the crew leapt from the bow holding a painter to make her fast. With a jump of his heart Paris read the words painted above the eye on the scarlet prow. The name sprang in a whisper to his lips: *Helen of Sparta*.

Phereclus heard it and grunted, 'A good name for a pretty little craft!'

'She's more than pretty,' Paris said, 'she's beautiful!'

Almost without volition he fell to his knees, pressed a hand to his mouth, and then touched it to the lips of the figurehead where the goddess lay on an ox-cart, nestling the infant Eros at her breast. With his eyes briefly closed, and his mind on fire, Paris made a silent prayer of thanks.

Looking back at the ship again, he saw a tall man in a tunic of white linen standing at the bow, fanning himself with a sun hat as he stared ashore. His hair glowed like a beacon in the ruddy light of the late afternoon.

By now all the men working on the ship had downed their tools. Most of them were gazing in a mixture of admiration and apprehension at the foreign vessel, though one or two looked back at the city where a company of armed horsemen were already passing through the gates on their way to the shore.

'What business does an Argive have in Trojan waters?' Paris called.

'Peaceful business, and holy,' the red-haired man answered. 'I come here as a supplicant.'

Paris saw the long scar left by a sword across the man's cheek. He said, 'To beg forgiveness for the towns you've raided and burned?'

'Not I, friend,' the man smiled. 'I'm no pirate. My name is Menelaus, King of Sparta.' He glanced quickly askance at the approaching troop.

Again Paris felt his heart lurch. 'And husband to the lady for whom your ship is named?'

'I have that honour.'

'And with it every man's envy, I understand.'

Menelaus dipped his head in a courteous smile of acknowlededgement. 'My wife will be flattered to learn that rumour of her beauty has travelled so far.'

'If you live to return to her.' Paris kept his voice light, covering the agitation of his heart. 'You still haven't told us what you want here.'

'I come at the bidding of the Delphic oracle. My country is afflicted with a plague that will lift only when I offer sacrifice at the tombs of Lycus and Chimaerus. I'm told they lie on Trojan land, near Apollo's shrine at Sminthe.'

A pang of guilt seared through Paris. He was thinking of Oenone and of the many times he and she had returned together to visit her father Cebren at Apollo's shrine.

But, 'I know the place,' he said. 'I used to raise bulls not far from there.'

'Then the gods are with me. Guide me there, herdsman, and I will pay you well, both for that service and for a hecatomb of your finest animals.'

Paris smiled at him. 'You'll need my father's permission first.'

'Is this your father?'

'No, this is Phereclus, son of Tecton, the most skilful shipwright in all Asia. My father is Priam, King of Troy, and this—' Paris smiled in the direction of the approaching horsemen '—is his palace guard coming to arrest you.'

Menelaus held up his hands. 'Forgive my mistake, Prince of Troy. It was an honest one – though I might have guessed as much from your noble bearing. Will you inform your men that I come in peace and am quite unarmed?'

'Do you swear to that?'

'I do.'

'On your wife's life?'

'That is a fearful oath – but yes, on my wife's life.'

'Then consider yourself under my protection, friend. My name is Paris, though some men call me Alexander. Be welcome here in Troy.'

With a prayer of thanks for a safe voyage, Menelaus leapt down from his ship and waded ashore through the surf. He was offering his hand to Paris as the troop of horsemen cantered up, led by

Antiphus who shouted a challenge at the stranger from under his high-plumed helmet.

Paris smiled up at him. 'We are honoured to entertain the King of Sparta in our city, brother. Before your men get too excited, tell them to lower their arms and lend a hand to haul this lovely ship inshore. I have taken Menelaus under my protection. His royal person is sacred, both as a holy supplicant here and as the guest of my house.'

True to his word, Paris took Menelaus into his own richly furnished apartment at the palace and placed himself as a buffer between his guest and the polite but suspicious way in which most of his brothers received the Spartan king within their walls. It was Paris too who conducted Menelaus into the presence of King Priam the next day, where he explained the urgent reason for this unannounced mission to Troy.

'Far-sighted Apollo is revered here in Troy,' Priam answered gravely. 'If his oracle sends you, son of Atreus, then be welcome among us. The holy place you seek lies on the Dardanian lands of my royal cousin Anchises, whom you have already met at Telamon's court. He speaks well of you and we value his wise counsel. No doubt his son Aeneas will conduct you to the tombs.'

'Gladly,' said Aeneas, 'and Paris will help us choose the bulls for sacrifice.'

'Then take the animals as our gift,' said Priam. 'Now come, Sparta. You and I must talk of other things. I have a sister who was carried away from us in an evil time and dearly wishes to return. Telamon listens neither to her pleas nor to my demands, but he does listen to your brother. Do you not think it would be well if Agamemnon and I were of the same mind on this matter?'

'My own wife, Helen, was abducted once,' Menelaus answered. 'We understand your sister's suffering, and your own concern.'

'Then you will help us in this matter?'

'Telamon is certain of the justice of his case,' said Menelaus quietly.

'And of the power of your brother's armies.'

'I am sure,' Menelaus smiled, 'that the High King of Troy also protects his friends and allies.'

'He does,' said Priam, 'should need arise. Do you anticipate such need?'

Menelaus considered for a moment before answering. 'Telamon's quarrels are not of immediate concern to me. At a time of pestilence, my thoughts lie only with the welfare of my family and country.'

'But if Agamemnon were to go to war,' Deiphobus taunted, 'would you let your wife keep you in her bed?'

'The King of Sparta is our guest,' Paris intervened. 'He deserves our courtesy. I am sure he would be as ready as I am to come to a brother's aid.'

'As I am to my sister's also,' said Priam. 'We will all fight for our own if need be.' He studied the Spartan king with narrowed eyes. 'Lord Menelaus, ours has long been a peaceful kingdom, but be in no doubt about our resolve. When you return to Argos, tell your brother that you have found Troy to be a strong and powerful city, one which prefers a reasoned solution to its conflicts. But tell him also that we will not hesitate to use her might should reason fail.'

Menelaus nodded. 'Then let us trust that with Apollo's guidance, reason will prevail. Such is my own earnest wish.'

The High King permitted himself a smile. 'I see that our son Paris has found good cause to make you his friend. It was brave to come here as you have, unarmed, but it was also wise. May Apollo the Healer take you under his protection and find your offerings acceptable.'

A banquet was thrown for the Spartan king that night, but he ate sparely and drank only water in order to remain cleansed for the forthcoming act of sacrifice. The most sober man at the feast, he replied with good humour to the occasional taunt and the many remarks about the enviable beauty of his wife.

'Can it be true what the minstrels say,' asked Aeneas, 'that she was hatched out of a swan's egg?'

'As true as what the minstrels say of your father,' Menelaus answered. 'That he was blinded by Aphrodite for boasting that he had lain with her!'

'Then you do not believe that I am Aphrodite's son?'

'As surely as I believe my wife to be Zeus's daughter.'

'Ah, but how sure is that?'

'As sure as I am that Helen's beauty – like your own manly form – has that about it which is certainly immortal.'

'Well answered, Sparta,' Hector put in, 'but as you see, I too have a desirable wife, and there are many beautiful women in this city. I dare wager that Asia has much to teach Argos in the arts of love. Can we not tempt you to try the skill of one of our Trojan beauties tonight?' He gestured to some of the young women sitting by the harper. They stood up, smiling, to make a show of themselves.

'An enticing offer, friend Hector,' Menelaus answered, 'but I trust you will understand that I mean no disrespect when I say that it is not only my condition as a supplicant that bids me decline.'

'And a man who lies nightly with Helen,' Paris supplied for his embarrassed friend, 'can want for no other in his bed.' He glanced at Menelaus, took a swig of spiced wine from his cup, and said, 'I would dearly love to look upon such beauty.'

'Then one day you must come to Sparta and I will entertain you there as royally as you have received me here. I know that my wife would wish to thank you in particular, Paris, for taking me so readily under your protection. Helen was fearful that I might find a colder welcome here in Troy.'

At that moment Cassandra rose from where she had been listening in rapt silence to the men's banter. She stood swaying for a moment with one hand held to her temple, then hissed across the table, 'Not cold, Atreides Menelaus – not cold but the heat of smoking flames awaits the Argive host in Troy. I have seen them writhe like serpents from a mouth that suckled on a bear. I have watched them lick and spread and burst untrammelled through the windows and the doors.' Andromache and her serving-women were already rising to escort Cassandra away, but the struggling girl was still shouting as they dragged her from the hall. 'Keep a close watch on your hearth, King of Sparta, or a serpent will steal fire from it that will set the world ablaze.'

When he saw Menelaus involuntarily making the sign to ward off the evil eye, Hector hastened to reassure him. 'You must forgive my sister. Since Apollo rejected her as his priestess she has been troubled in her mind. I beg you to think nothing of what she has said. It is only such craziness as she is often wont to utter.'

Menelaus had seen from the girl's upturned eyes and the harrowed darkness of her young features that all was not well with her. So though he had been startled by the outburst, he was ready to dismiss it. 'Please,' he said, 'my own family has known madness enough in its time. There is no need to apologize.'

But the conviviality of the evening had been dispelled and could not easily be recovered. After a time Menelaus yawned and got to his feet. 'You must forgive me, lords, but the hour grows late. Tomorrow I must perform my sacred duties, and right now I am much in need of sleep.'

'Come,' said Paris, 'I will accompany you from the hall. Tomorrow I will show you the beauty of our land.' He clapped a hand to his guest's back. 'And – who knows? – perhaps one day soon you will show me the beauty of yours.'

Yet Paris did not lie easily in his bed that night.

Ever since Aphrodite had promised to make Helen his wife, he had made a daily offering to the goddess. Each day, as the smoke rose and the doves flew about her statue, his offering had been accompanied by a fervent prayer that she remember her pledge and show him the way by which the path of his life might cross with that of the most beautiful woman in the world. At first sight, therefore, he had been certain that Menelaus must have come to Troy through the agency of Aphrodite. But the more he had come to know of the Spartan king the more he grew to like the man, and the less sure he became.

When Paris had first conceived the idea of carrying off Helen in a pirate raid, Menelaus had been no more than a name to him, and the name, moreover, of a likely enemy of Troy. The idea of stealing such a man's wife presented no difficulties. But he and Menelaus were no longer strangers, and Paris was finding it impossible not to respect and admire the noble-hearted man who had come so unexpectedly as a supplicant to Troy.

Already, on that first day, he and Aeneas had welcomed Menelaus more warmly and with less overt suspicion than had many others in Priam's court. By the end of the following day, after they had ridden out to the lands around Mount Ida with him, the three men were bonded in firm friendship.

Menelaus listened as Paris told him of the early years in which he had been raised as a herdsman in those parts, and warmly commended the courage with which, as a mere boy, he had fought off the gang of Argive cattle-lifters. In turn, the Spartan king spoke about the dark time of his own boyhood as a younger brother in the violent turmoil of the house of Atreus. So by the time Paris had escorted Menelaus to the mountain pastures of his youth and helped him to select the best bulls for the sacrifice, he was wondering how, in all conscience, he could ever permit himself to betray the trust of a man with such an open and generous nature? Yet without such betrayal he could never possess the woman whose face obsessed his heart.

There were many reasons, therefore, why he decided not to accompany Menelaus on the last stage of his journey to Apollo's shrine at Sminthe. Not the least of them were his qualms at the prospect of encountering Oenone. On many occasions since his arrival in Troy, Paris had intended to send her a message and each time he had failed to do so. With each failure it became more difficult even to think about her, and whenever he did so the memory of her face was instantly displaced by the image of

Helen. The truth was that Paris had shuffled off his previous life much as a snake sloughs its skin and the thought of the people he had wronged in this way left him uneasy with guilt. Above all this was true of Oenone. Suspecting that her love had proved more enduring than his own, he told himself it would be wiser to avoid her company rather than risk opening a wound that must surely by now have begun to heal. So with the excuse that he wished to spend some time with his foster-father Agelaus and the friends of his youth, he left Aeneas to act as guide to the shrine. Not long afterwards, having found himself no longer at ease among the herdsmen, he returned to wait for Menelaus and Aeneas in the palace of Anchises at Lyrnessus under Mount Ida.

Paris dined alone with the Dardanian king that night, but after the first exchange of courtesies, the silence between them was so prolonged that he began to wonder whether Anchises was disdainful of his company. After all, as this day had reminded him, he had once been no more than a herdsman on the blind king's land. Priam might have taken him warmly to his heart and required all Troy to do the same, but here in Dardania it seemed that Paris felt comfortable neither in the royal palace nor in the hovels of the herdsmen. Having trifled with his food, he was contemplating the various occasions he had given himself for shame, when Anchises turned abruptly from drying his hands after the meal and astonished him by saying, 'Come closer, boy. Let these hands have sight of your face.'

Apprehensively, Paris did as he was bidden. He sat staring into the dark sockets of a head that might have been carved from olive-wood as Anchises's fingers travelled across the contours of his face, pressing the eyelids, probing the lines of his mouth. Never in his life had he felt so intimately perceived. He had to fight the impulse to pull away, for it felt as if that powerful and sensitive touch must uncover every secret of his heart.

Eventually Anchises lowered his hands. 'I see it is true what they say. The gods have gifted you with great beauty, boy.' After a pensive moment he added, 'There is a fate that comes with such a gift.'

'Each man must meet the fate that he is given,' Paris answered, sensing that more was to come.

The older man nodded. 'They tell me that you devote yourself to Aphrodite over all the other gods.'

'A man must also choose.'

Again there was a long silence. Anchises fumbled with his right hand for the gold-mounted staff that he had left leaning against the wall at his back. Thinking that he meant to get up, Paris moved to help him but the old king gestured him away. Having found his staff, he sat with both hands over its pommel, and the jut of his chin resting on his hands. His face was turned towards the heat of the fire.

'In my youth,' he said quietly, 'I too abandoned myself to Aphrodite.'

Paris waited. For several moments Anchises seemed lost in thought, as though that distant past was more vivid to him than the darkness of this docile present. Then he turned his fierce blind gaze towards the place where Paris sat in tense anticipation. 'As you see,' he said, 'I found her a stern mistress.' He uttered a small, derisory sigh and turned that blighted face back towards the hearth before he added, almost as an afterthought, 'I would not wish to have you blinded by her too.'

Uncertain how to respond, Paris said, 'I believe she means well by me.'

'Perhaps.' Anchises scraped the bronze ferrule of his staff across the stones of the hearth. 'But there is more than one way to be blind.'

'Then I shall try to keep my eyes open.'

Paris had uttered the remark as lightly as he dared, but Anchises did not smile. Tapping his stick just once against the stone, he said, 'Are you listening to me, boy?'

Paris had jumped and nodded before he remembered that he could not be seen. 'I am,' he said softly.

'Then hear what I would not hear when I was young as you are, and just as sure of my own destiny.' Again Anchises tapped his stick once, sharply, on the stone hearth. 'Serve Aphrodite if it is your fate to do so. Serve her well. But remember she is not alone among the gods. *Nothing in extreme*, do you hear? That is the wisdom of Apollo. Nothing too much – not even in reverence for the goddess who has chosen you.'

The fire hissed on its stones. Somewhere outside the hall, the chamberlain was berating a slave in angry whispers. 'Do you hear me?' Anchises demanded again. And Paris, who had been reflecting that this old man must also have been arrogantly handsome once, said, 'I hear you, uncle.'

'Do you?' The blind king muttered without turning his head. 'Do you indeed?'

Nothing further was said. After a time, without explanation or apology, the old man got to his feet, called for his body-servant, and made his way to bed.

Paris sat up alone over his wine for a long time, brooding, drinking too much. His mood darkened. More gravely than at any time since he had come down from Mount Ida, he was troubled by doubts about the destiny which Aphrodite had promised him.

On the following night, Menelaus returned to Anchises's palace with Aeneas, having performed his acts of sacrifice at the tombs of Lycus and Chimaerus. He was exhausted but also glowing with exaltation, for he had been given clear signs that his offerings were found acceptable in the sight of the god. Aeneas insisted that they must banquet in celebration, and the three friends laughed often as they ate well and drank heavily together. Then Anchises, who had remained silent throughout most of the meal, tapped his staff and commanded his minstrel to sing the Lay of Troy.

With a quick, apologetic glance at his guest, Aeneas deferentially suggested that it had been a hard day and the lay might prove a little long and solemn for the occasion. But Anchises was insistent, and Menelaus politely averred that he would like to learn more of the land's ancestral history. Fortunately, the old minstrel's voice was still strong, and his touch on the harp proud and skilful.

The song told how the country south of the Hellespont had first been settled under the aegis of Apollo by Teucer, who had come to Phrygia from Athens. Then Dardanus had come there out of Arcadia and built a town on the lower slopes of Mount Ida. It was his grandson Tros who had given his name to the land, and *his* son, Ilus, who brought the Palladium – the ancient image of Pallas Athena – to the hill of Ate, where the citadel of Ilium was founded. Around that sacred precinct had grown the noble city of Troy itself. The song climaxed with an account of how Earth-shaker Poseidon had punished the impiety of Laomedon by destroying the city, which had then been sacked by Heracles and Telamon. The minstrel concluded his lay with a paean of praise for the way the High King Priam and his royal cousin Anchises, had restored the glory of the land and added to its riches.

'I tried to warn Laomedon of his folly,' Anchises sighed when the song had ended, 'but he would not listen. We Dardanians are a peaceful people. Though we will fight in a just cause, we prefer to hunt and breed good bulls and tend our herds.' He shook his head. 'I have smelled the dead in a burning city once. I have no wish to do so again.'

Menelaus raised his goblet. 'Then let us hope you never have to, my friend.'

'But that intransigent fool Telamon still lives,' Anchises said grimly, 'and he is no friend to Troy.' He turned his head in the direction from which Menelaus's voice had come. 'Nor, I think, is your brother.'

There was an uneasy moment of silence, which Paris was about to break when Anchises raised his hand and spoke again. 'Hear me, Menelaus. When Antenor and I were on Salamis, I listened carefully to you and your brother. Of the two sons of Atreus, I am convinced that the mind of Menelaus is more amenable to reason than that of Agamemnon. One might wish that it was you, not he, who sits on the high throne at Mycenae.'

'My brother knows that I am content in Sparta,' Menelaus warily replied.

Anchises nodded. 'But he would do well to listen to your sober counsel. And all the more so now that you know us and have seen our strength. Let us think about this together, friend. My cousin Priam has a great love for his sister. After all, he owes his very life to her. Also his heart is hasty, and where Hesione's fate is concerned, he is ready to let it overrule his head. Does it not seem to you, as it does to me, that if Priam and Agamemnon are left to their own devices, they will drag us into a war that neither you nor I, nor any reasonable man desires? Might it not be wise to temper their hot spirits with our own cooler reflections?'

Aware that the others were listening keenly for his response, Menelaus said quietly, 'What do you have in mind?'

Anchises sat in silence by the fire for a time before answering. 'My nephew Paris and my son Aeneas have proposed to make a voyage to Argos soon. Could they not build on the friendship that we have made here tonight? If you will speak privily to Agamemnon – as I will to Priam – then might he not be persuaded to receive them as ambassadors of peace and mutual prosperity rather than harbingers of war? Surely it would be in all our interests for him to blunt Telamon's horns rather than letting him rage far beyond his paddock?'

Now it was Menelaus who took time to consider his answer. He remembered how deeply Helen had dreaded the thought of war, and how sorely Sparta stood in need of a time of peace to recover from the ravages of plague. He reflected on how generously he had been received in the Trojan lands, and how fond he had grown, in so brief a time, of his new friends, Paris and Aeneas. He was filled with admiration for everything Priam had achieved in Troy, and with respect for the blind Dardanian king's appraisal of the situation. So when he searched his heart he could find no appetite for warfare – only the desire to rule over a peaceable kingdom with his beloved wife beside him.

'I think that you and I are of the same mind,' he said at last. 'I will speak with Agamemnon on my return and tell him what kindness and wisdom I have met with here. As for my two noble companions—' he smiled at Paris and Aeneas '—they have become dear friends and will receive the warmest of welcomes in Sparta at least. We shall see what transpires when I present them as ambassadors before the High King in Mycenae.'

Like a sudden alteration in the weather, the tension in the room dispersed.

'Then let it be a time for new beginnings,' said Anchises. 'Let us hope that youth and vigour can succeed where Antenor and I have failed.'

Aeneas lifted his cup to pledge the hope. After the others joined him, his father retired, and though the three of them were already drunk, Aeneas insisted that ten years was long enough for wine to stand and called for more. Soon they were drunker, and ready to swear undying friendship.

'Come to Argos,' Menelaus was already slurring his words, 'and I will show you . . . I will show you . . .' He blinked at Paris. 'Tell me, my handsome friend, what do you love most in all the world?'

'Bulls!' Aeneas said, and started chuckling. 'He loves bulls.'

'No, no,' Paris demurred woozily, 'that was all a long time ago.'

'But you're still a bull-fancier,' Aeneas insisted. 'You saw him fondling those monsters yesterday, Menelaus. He likes them meaty and big. The bigger the better. Be sure that if Argos has bulls to tame, our Paris is the man for it.'

'No,' Menelaus laughed. 'I think he's more interested in women! I think he's a heart-breaker as well as a bull-breaker.'

Aeneas wagged a tipsy finger at Paris. 'That reminds me. We came across a pretty little thing wandering by the Scamander yesterday. She asked after you rather tenderly. Can't recall her

name, but she called you Alexander. Do you remember her? Or
have there been too many others since then?'

Paris stared at his friend. Quite suddenly his heart had capsized
and was tipping him out of drunkenness into misery.

'Oenone,' he said. 'Her name's Oenone.'

'So hers was the first heart you broke!' Aeneas shook his head
in mock reproof. 'Ah well, she'll have more to remember you by
than the others. She's big with child.' When he saw how Paris's
face had blanched at the news, he added cheerfully, 'Don't worry,
it won't be the first fatherless brat in Dardania. And I'm sure
you'll leave lots of other by-blows in your wake, like your father
before you. No doubt they'll all claim they're sons of a god!'
Then Menelaus and Aeneas were chuckling together, the dispro-
portionate laughter of tired and drunken men enjoying the spec-
tacle of a friend on the run.

'Oh dear, we seem to have fingered a wound,' Aeneas said. 'I
think she must have been his first love!'

'Is that right, Paris?' Menelaus asked more gently. 'Was she your
first sweetheart – as Helen was mine?'

Paris glanced away. 'It was the herdsman who loved her, not
the prince.'

'And for this prince,' Aeneas winked at Menelaus, 'there will
be many others. What else should one expect from a devotee of
the Golden One?'

Menelaus smiled benevolently at Paris. 'The Golden One, eh?
Well, the Goddess Who Loves Laughter has beguiling powers, I
grant you, but you can burn yourself at her altar. If you are wise
you will follow my example. My service is to Athena and to
Hera, and I've found great contentment there. Take a good wife,
Paris. That's what you need to steady you. A good wife. Do it as
soon as you can. A man can look for no surer foundation to his
fortunes.'

'But in that respect,' Aeneas snorted, 'you're the envy of the
world. Any man would be content if he knew that Helen lay
waiting in his bed. Isn't that right, Paris?'

'If everything they say of her is true.'

'Oh, it's true all right!' Menelaus smiled. 'Had you the patience for it, friends, I could sing Helen's praises far into the night. But what is the point when words cannot match her beauty and you'll soon be in Sparta to judge for yourselves?' He stared deeply into his wine-cup, smiling fondly, as though seeing his wife's reflection there. 'In fact, I'm so sure you'll find her the loveliest creature you've ever set eyes on that I'd stake my life and happiness on it.'

'But wouldn't that be to lose Helen herself?' Aeneas laughed.

Menelaus opened his free hand. 'My point exactly,' and his bleary eyes beamed at Paris over the rim of his goblet with the serene satisfaction of one who knows himself privileged to be the most fortunate of men.

The Trojan Embassy

In the weeks before he sailed to Sparta, Paris endured a deeply
unsettling time. It began on the morning of the day after Menelaus
had made his sacrifices at the ancient burial mounds. Rather than
returning at once to Troy, Aeneas had suggested that he and Paris
take their guest hunting through the chasms of the Idaean mountains where boar were plentiful and bears and lion might still be
found. They had chanced on one of the largest boars that any of
them had ever seen, a bristling hunk of animal flesh, long-tusked
and as nimble as it was muscular. By the time the men came up
the blind ravine where the hounds had bayed it, the boar had
torn the guts from two dogs, trampled another and unnerved the
rest. It stood in dappled light, bleeding from one ear. Paris and
Aeneas stood aside, inviting their guest to make the kill. But the
boar was not yet ready to die. Even as Menelaus raised his spear,
it swerved and lunged for the cover of a thicket to vanish in
green shade.

A steep wall of rock rose beyond the undergrowth, preventing
escape, so the hunters knew the animal must be lurking nearby.
As Paris used his knife to cut the windpipe of a yelping dog,
Aeneas whistled in the two remaining hounds, but they had heard
the death gasp of their comrade, and had learned too much of
this uncanny boar's ferocity and cunning to risk its frenzy in a

confined space. Aeneas was impatiently urging them on when, from an entirely unexpected quarter, the boar made its break. It came crashing out of the thicket, driving its ferocious bulk directly at Aeneas, who lost his footing as he turned, and would have been gored in the belly if Menelaus had not loosed his spear in time to bring the beast down in a gush of blood across the legs of the Dardanian prince. The boar lay there, wheezing out its last breaths under the weight of the long shaft, blinking sullenly at death.

Aeneas came out of the scrape with no more than a gashed calf, and was already laughing as he thanked Menelaus for a timely throw. But Paris had seen everything from where he knelt above the dead dog with the knife in his hand and his spear lying useless on the ground beside him. He was watching still as Menelaus tore a strip from his own tunic to bind the wounded leg. He heard the jocular remarks they made without listening to them, for the day had fallen still around him, and he was struck by a numbing sense that everything of which he had once dreamed was now impossible. Already he had been troubled by the growing warmth of his affection for the Spartan king. Now he owed to that noble-hearted man the life of his dearest friend, and it had become unthinkable to contemplate betraying Menelaus by making off with the wife he so manifestly worshipped.

Paris saw that he had been living for too long with an illusion. His vision of the goddesses on Mount Ida could have been no more than an idle dream brought on by drowsiness and solitude. Now he was awake in the world again, and the world was suddenly a colder place.

The hunters returned to Troy that night, and the *Helen of Sparta* put out into the Hellespont two mornings later. But even before Menelaus had left to return to his beloved wife, Paris had begun to give over his own nights to a frenzy of love-making among the women of the city. Life had forbidden him to take what he had once dreamed that Aphrodite had offered him. Very well! If Helen was not to be his, he would renounce his foolish abstinence and take advantage of all the other women that the goddess placed at his disposal.

There were many of them.

The lovesick daughters of Troy found his passionate exploration of their young bodies more heartbreaking than his earlier vow of chastity had been, for his interest rarely lasted longer than a night or two. Their coyness lacked the wild innocence he had once loved in Oenone, and he soon tired of their claims and complaints and tears. After one bitter encounter with a young woman whose sultry demeanour was matched only by her temper, he seriously considered turning his back on the city and seeking out Oenone and the child she carried. But the thought of resuming a narrow life among the Dardanian cattle-herders held little appeal now that the whole world stood open to him, and he knew that Oenone would never be at ease among the painted and perfumed women of the Trojan court. So he turned to the courtesans of the city, and from them he swiftly learned the arts that turned him from an ardent animal into a skilful lover. Soon he was making assignations with those wives of worthy Trojan burghers who had made plain their amorous interest in him. The secrecy of these liaisons gave them an air of excitement for a time, particularly when he was juggling three women at once, none of whom knew that he was bedding the others, but it wasn't long before he was filled with self-loathing at his own duplicity. He was aware too that, as he grew more careless, he was making enemies among the men he cuckolded, and though his position as the High King's favoured son might stave off any open challenge, it would not protect him from a hired knife in the dark.

Dismayed by these unaccountable changes in his behaviour, Aeneas warned him of the risks he was running, yet Paris merely shrugged off his friend's concern. With no guiding vision left to direct his life, he had more or less resigned himself to a brief career of meaningless sensual pleasure when he was approached one evening by Hector's wife, Andromache. She reminded Paris that she had always been among his well-wishers, that she had rejoiced with Priam and Hecuba at the return of their lost son, and that she and Hector had entertained high hopes that he would bring fresh energy to the king's council and prove a stalwart defender of the city and its interests. Imagine their dismay, therefore, to watch him waste his youth and vigour in a dissolute life of reprehensible affairs. What had become of the native dignity he had brought with him from the mountains? It was natural enough that a young man had wild oats to sow, but Paris was in danger of offending all propriety and of throwing his life away. Did he imagine that such licentiousness was consonant with a proper devotion to love's service? Could she not prevail on him to ease the anxiety of his mother's heart by mending his ways?

Andromache left Paris overwhelmed by remorse. He vowed to himself that he would renew his interest in the political life of Troy and take a responsible role in the life of his family. He began to attend his father's court again, trying to understand the complex web of treaties and trade agreements that under-pinned the prosperity of the city. And he gave some of his leisure hours to sporting with his little brother Capys and his playmate Antheus, who was the son of Antenor, the king's chief counsellor. Finding in the boys some echo of his own lost innocence, Paris would lead them on expeditions to the rivers and the mountains, where he excited their young hearts with tales of the hunt or of fighting bulls, and of how, as a boy, he had driven off the Argive rustlers.

One day, near the end of the summer, they accompanied him to the shore for a last consultation with Phereclus about his ship, the *Aphrodite*, which stood complete now in everything but her final details. Paris had drunk too much wine the night before and his head was aching still, so he took little pleasure in visiting a ship that had now lost almost all purpose for him. As the boys clambered aboard and ran about the deck, playing at pirates with their wooden swords, Paris looked up into the eyes of the figure-head and felt a wave of yearning for the days when this was still a ship of dreams, not just the vessel which would shortly take him on a sober diplomatic journey to the Argive kingdoms. In the past hectic weeks, he'd tried to extinguish the vision of Helen from his mind, but the exquisitely carved face of Aphrodite smiled down from the prow with superior knowledge, and he knew the vision was inextinguishable. He would sail to Sparta and find Helen, yes. But the Helen he found would be the loyal wife of his friend, and would remain what she had always been – a forever unattainable fantasy of his restless heart.

The accident happened so abruptly that he was never quite sure afterwards how it had come about. He had been arguing with Phereclus over some minor detail in the way the after-awning was rigged. They were already shouting above the noise of saws and hammers from the other boats in the yard where Priam's fleet was under construction, when the boys came towards them, clattering their wooden swords together as they jumped from oar-bench to oar-bench, whooping out their battle-cries. Paris told them to make less noise, which they did for a moment, but Antheus poked Capys with his sword and soon their shrill voices were hooting out battlefield insults at each other. Then they were fighting their way back down the benches again, shouting as they came.

In a fit of anger, Paris shouted, 'Didn't I tell you to keep quiet?', and swung his arm to cuff the nearest boy across the ear. The blow landed harder than he intended, Antheus was knocked off the bench from which he had been about to leap and fell, twisting, to the deck below. His thin right arm hit the boards first, bending under the impact in such a way that the wooden sword turned in his grip and entered the socket of his eye. The force of the fall was strong enough to drive the point into his brain.

Paris looked down where the boy's skinny body lay crumpled in a widening pool of blood with his head propped at an improbable angle on the sword. He looked up and saw Phereclus staring wide-eyed. Beside him, with the fingers of one hand pushed into his mouth, Capys gazed down in puzzled dismay at his dead friend.

★ ★ ★

No one doubted that the death of Antheus was an accident, and no one could doubt that Paris was responsible for it. Antheus had been the youngest, much spoiled son of Antenor, and neither the king's counsellor nor his wife, Theano, who was high-priestess to Athena in the city, could bring themselves even to look at Paris in the days after he carried their child's dead body back to them.

Nor could the grief-stricken parents find the forgiveness to cleanse him of his guilt, and no one else in the city had the power to do so. Unable to clear his mind of the dead child's ruined face, or to silence the sound of Theano's wailing in his ears, Paris lay awake at night, agonized by remorse, and with the Furies screeching through the darkness round him.

It seemed that his whole life amounted to no more than a vain tissue of futility and betrayal. He had neglected the foster-parents who had reared him, forsaken Oenone and the child she carried, toyed with the hearts of more women than he could recall, and cuckolded many good citizens of Troy. Worst of all, he had disavowed the vision that had once filled his life with meaning, and because of that he had now caused the death of a child – a deed terrible in itself, and one which added to the grievances that Athena held against him. Perhaps the priest and priestess of Apollo had been right all those years ago and his life was cursed from the start?

The one saving thought was that he and Aeneas would shortly set sail for Sparta. Somewhere out there on the blue ocean, far beyond the only horizon he had ever known, he must find a way either to redeem his afflicted life or to meet whatever end the gods intended for it.

On the night before he was due to sail, his father summoned him to his private chamber. King Priam sat in the chair he had rescued from the burning embers of his father's palace in Troy many years before – a flame-blackened throne that he kept as a reminder of Laomedon's folly and the justice of the gods. Around his shoulders he wore a richly embroidered cloak that was fastened

at his chest by a gold chain and clasp, figured with strange, mutu-
ally devouring beasts that some Thracian goldsmith had worked
for him. The flat of one bony hand supported his chin. The other,
gorgeously ringed, trembled where it lay against his thigh. He
looked, and felt, very old.

'It grieves my heart to think that you must put to sea unpu-
rified,' he sighed. 'Believe me, I know what it is like to lose a
son, but I was luckier than Antenor. His child can never be
restored to him. And the blow that killed Antheus has hardened
his father's heart. I greatly fear that your rash act has made my
old friend and counsellor your enemy for the remainder of his
days.'

Priam's eyes glanced away across the chamber. Paris merely
nodded his head in assent to the judgement. Then his father
added wearily, 'And Antenor may not be the only one. There
have been murmurings in the city. My spies tell me there are
husbands who say that it is one thing to be a devotee of Aphrodite,
but another to sacrifice the lives of children on her altar.'

Paris gasped and was about to protest when Priam silenced
him. 'The death of Antheus was an unhappy chance, I know. But
men will look for the hand of a god behind such things, and
you have taken many risks in service to the Golden One. It is
well that you are going from Troy right now. But we must take
thought for your return.'

'If this city tires of me I will remain abroad,' Paris answered
sullenly. 'There are even those among my brothers who will be
glad to see my back.'

'Then do not play the proud fool with the father who loves
you.' Priam shook his head. 'It is time your passions were bridled
by cool thought. Consider this: Antenor has always opposed my
plans for an assault on Salamis. He fears that to attack Telamon
would bring down the whole Argive host upon this city, and he
could be right. So you may do something to redeem yourself in
his eyes, if you can secure a treaty of peace with Agamemnon
through your friendship with the King of Sparta.' Priam drew

his breath in a deep sigh. 'I am not hopeful of it. The Mycenaean lion has been growing hungry and proud for some time now. I think he smells fat prey in Troy, and it will take more than subtle words to keep him from our gates. But see what can be done, my son. And if – as I predict – Agamemnon remains intransigent over the fate of my dear sister . . . well, remember that once you had another plan.'

The eyes of the two men met for a moment in the oil-lamp's unsteady light. The air of the chamber was very still. In its silence Priam licensed his son, if all else failed, to use the gifts the gods had given him, as lover and as warrior, to make off with some Argive princess that they might hold as hostage for the ransom of Hesione.

'I remember very well, father,' Paris answered. But what he remembered brought only a further pang of anguish to his troubled heart.

He knelt, dully, to receive his father's blessing. Priam laid both his hands across his bowed head and looked down at his son. 'One thing more occurs to me. Menelaus is a sacred king in Sparta. He has priestly powers, he is your friend and he stands in our debt. By permitting him to offer sacrifices in Dardania we enabled him to cleanse his own land of pestilence. As a true king he will not have forgotten this. So when he makes his offerings at the temple of Athena in Sparta, kneel before him as you kneel now before me, and ask him to cleanse you of the impurity that haunts your mind. Though Athena's priestess here in Ilium now carries only hatred in her heart for you, the goddess herself is merciful. Menelaus will not refuse you. May the gods go with you, and bring you safely home.'

The two ships put out at dawn, Paris in the *Aphrodite* and Aeneas in his own vessel, the *Gorgona*. At first the air was so still that the crews had to take to the oars, but as the day brightened, a breeze got up, and soon the two ships were cutting under sail through white-capped waves while dolphins plunged and shone about them. The pale blur of the coastline at their backs dropped below the horizon, and they were racing into open sea. Leaving his ship-master to watch the helm, Paris stood alone at the prow, taking the bright spray from the bow wave in his face and staring ahead into the blue-green glitter of the day. Hours passed without him uttering a word, and later, by night, he lay far from sleep on the afterdeck, gazing up into the steep black deeps where count-less stars tipped and swirled about the tinkling masthead. The voyage itself was quickly proving restorative. With each dip and surge of the ship he felt the shadows of Troy fall from him, as though he was quietly decanting the past from his soul in order to fill it with a future.

As he watched the surf break in spindrift at the bow, or fall shimmering off a dolphin's back, he was thinking of Aphrodite and how the goddess had taken her name from the white curdle of foam in which her naked beauty was born.

So he was following her now through her native element. She was both the vessel that bore him and the foam on which it floated, and her presence was manifest in the quick glances of the shining breeze and the sparkling light that lifted off the sea. With the force of returning memory it came clear to him again that in the same moment that he had chosen her, Aphrodite had chosen him, and he was held as securely in her embrace as was the infant Eros figured in her arms at the prow of the ship that bore her sacred name.

Yet that thought brought the picture of little Antheus back to his mind. His soul was not yet cleansed of that death, but he would submit himself in Sparta to the rites of purification, and once that was done he would be back inside his destiny again. If the blood of a child had been shed in his ship, then perhaps it had been a dreadful kind of sacrifice after all. For only through the death of innocence could his life be entirely consecrated to the service of that single-minded goddess, and he was utterly at her mercy now.

The realization came to him in almost the same moment that

a sailor at the yardarm of the *Gorgona* shouted that he had sighted land. Aeneas waved cheerily across the gap between the ships. Paris raised his own hand in reply.

They sailed among the islands off the coast of Attica, and across the uneventful waters of the Gulf of Argolis until they made landfall in a harbour on the Laconian coast. As the yardarm of the *Aphrodite* creaked down and the ship nudged her way towards the strand, Paris stood at the prow with both arms holding the painted figurehead of the goddess. He was looking north-eastwards to the rampart of mountains ringing the Spartan plain. Somewhere beyond those summits, not more than twenty miles away, lay the palace of Menelaus, and somewhere within its walls Helen would be going about her business, utterly unaware that an envoy sent by the goddess of love was thinking about her now, and with a heart that strummed as tautly as the full-bellied sail had done only moments before. The salt air quivered about his head. All his senses were alert. Each breath he took felt fresh with destiny. Yet strangely he felt more at peace with himself now than at any moment since Menelaus had sailed away from Troy. He had placed his life once more in the hands of the goddess. Aphrodite Pelagaia, She of the Fair Voyage, had brought him safely to Sparta. It was for her to decide his fate.

News of the arrival of the Trojan embassy reached the palace of Menelaus long before the visitors themselves came down through a high mountain pass to look upon the fertile plain of the Eurotas. To their amazement Paris and Aeneas saw how, beyond the rolling fields and groves, the city of Sparta stood unwalled. Though a gleaming acropolis crowned a low hill on the west bank of the river, the estates and houses of the city were scattered around it in small village communities across the valley floor with no apparent thought for their defence. Still further to the west, the late afternoon sun declined towards a range of mountains steeper than those through which their little cavalcade had just passed. Far beyond the tree-line, its summits reached for the burnished clouds, twice as high – Paris estimated in some awe – as his homeland mountain range of Ida.

With an ox-drawn wagon-load of gifts trundling behind them, the Trojans were following the river-road across the valley when a single chariot pulled by two black horses sped towards them from the city. The driver's red hair was blowing in the breeze, and long before the chariot skidded to a halt they had made out the burly, unarmed figure of Menelaus at the reins.

'I thought I should bid you welcome here in Sparta as informally as you once welcomed me to Troy, Paris,' he called. 'And you, friend Aeneas, do you recognize these horses? It's the pair your father gave me. Now they're the fastest team in all Argos. Even Agamemnon covets them. Come, leave your wagon to follow on – it'll be safe enough. Let's get you bathed and dined. My Lady Helen is impatient to meet my Trojan friends.' With a tug on the reins he wheeled his horses about, gesturing towards the citadel. 'Tell me, how do you like my land? Is it not beautiful?'

'Fairer even than I expected,' Paris answered, 'but Aeneas and I have been surprised to find that Sparta has no walls.'

'What need for walls,' Menelaus laughed, 'when the gods gave us this ring of mountains? Men think twice about invading Sparta when they know they will be cut down in the passes long before they set eyes on hollow Lacadaemon. My friends, you have entered the most contented kingdom in the world. What I have is yours to enjoy. I beg you to make free of it.'

In order that they might recover more easily from their journey, Menelaus had decided to spare his guests the demands of a public banquet that night, so they were to dine alone with the king and his wife in a private chamber. The Trojans soaked for a long time in hot baths and were massaged with aromatic oils by serving-women before being dressed in the fresh raiment put at their disposal. While they waited for the Queen of Sparta to appear, the two men strolled with their host through the nocturnal fragrance of a pleasure garden overlooking the city. They could see the river gleaming in the moonlight, and an expanse of olive-groves, orchards and wheat fields stretching away to the wooded foothills of the surrounding mountains.

When Aeneas turned to remark on the majestic pillared temple standing above the palace courtyard, Menelaus told him that he was looking at the Bronze House of Athena, the city's guardian deity.

Fearful that if he let this moment pass he might feel too com-promised to ask it later, Paris made a sign of respect and self-protection. 'Then I stand near the sacred ground of the goddess in trepidation. Without intending it, I have given offence to Grey-eyed Athena.' He took in his host's frown of concern and opened his hands. 'I have come to Sparta, as you once came to Priam's city, with a boon to crave.'

Menelaus put a hand to Paris's shoulder. 'Haven't I already said that what is mine is yours? Speak freely. Anything I can do for you shall surely be done.'

Paris drew in his breath. 'My father has counselled me to abase myself before you as Athena's sacred priest in Sparta, for in the eyes of the goddess – as in my own – I am still polluted by a crime. I beseech you to cleanse me of it in Athena's holy house by whatever rite you think proper.'

'This is bitter news,' Menelaus answered gravely. 'Come inside, friend, take more wine, and tell me what ill fate has fallen to you since we last met.'

The three men sat down together in the shifting light of many oil-lamps and Paris recounted the events of the day on which Antheus had died. 'The boy was the much-loved child of my father's counsellor Antenor, who is well known to you,' he ended. 'And the pity of it is he was scarcely five years old.'

'I remember Antenor fondly,' said Menelaus quietly. 'A wise man, whose judgement I respect. I grieve for his loss. And all the more so in that I have no son of my own. But how is it that this ill fortune has offended Athena?'

'Antenor's wife, Theano, is priestess to the goddess in her most sacred shrine at Troy. I have sworn on my own wretched life that the child's death was an accident, but there's no denying that the fault of it was mine, and Theano has hardened her heart against me. Since that day the Furies have roosted in my mind and no one at Troy can cleanse me of the guilt. I must carry it for ever unless your rites here in Sparta can free me of it.'

Paris looked up into the solemn eyes of his friend. Menelaus was about to answer him when a woman's voice spoke softly from the open door. 'Is this King Priam's son, my lord – he who gave you his protection when you first set foot in Troy?'

'It is, my lady, and this is his cousin Aeneas, son to the Dardanian King. My friend Prince Paris was just telling me . . .'

'I heard,' said Helen, 'and like yourself I was so rapt in his sad story that I was aware of nothing else.' Smiling softly at her husband, she added, 'Does our city not stand greatly in this prince's debt – as I most certainly do myself?'

Paris had already jumped to his feet. Now it felt as though the room was afloat as he stared at the thrilling beauty of this woman where she stood in the lamplight, wearing a simple dress of Tyrian blue that hung in graceful folds from the lines of her body. The dark fall of her hair was bound up in a golden fillet that seemed to brighten the blue-green of her eyes. Paris had forgotten how to breathe. Everything had vanished from his mind except the living presence of the woman he had seen in his vision on Mount Ida. And it was as if that moment and this were continuous in time, and the long space between of no more significance than so much sleep. Surely she too must feel the power of that confluence?

But if she did, Helen gave no sign, and somewhere in what had become the far distance he could hear Menelaus speaking. 'It does indeed, and we are mindful of it. I think my queen and I are already of one heart in this matter.'

Helen smiled. 'Then surely we must do all we can for our friend in his hour of need.'

But every thought of guilt and shame and grief had gone from Paris's mind.

He was standing awestruck in the presence of Helen of Sparta and he could hear the whisper of his goddess in the jasmine fragrance from the night outside. 'Is it not as I promised you?' she was saying. 'Was ever a lovelier woman seen across the surface of the earth?'

In the same instant he became aware that countless men before him must have looked on Helen's face in exactly this way. He sensed too that she had never learned how to respond easily to the unintended impact of her beauty, for he could see the confusion already gathering behind the tender solicitude in her eyes as she glanced away, smiling, and brought her hands together just below the white hollow of her throat in a demure gesture of self-protection that made his heart swim. When he looked back to her face he saw that the smile had swiftly withdrawn behind a mask of proud reserve – a pride he might have taken for arrogance had he not observed that earlier chink of vulnerability – and in those brief moments Paris knew that the rest of his life would be worth nothing unless he did everything in his power to make this woman his own.

'I see that all the minstrels' reports are true,' Aeneas was saying. 'The Lady Helen is as gracious as she is beautiful.'

Helen smiled at him, shaking her head. 'If you take the minstrels too seriously, Lord Aeneas, they will have you believing I was born from the eggshell of a swan!'

'Because such beauty is so rare,' Paris said in a hoarse whisper, 'that they must reach for figures to encompass it. And still they fail. As all the rich gifts that Troy has tried to find for you will also fail to match such grace.'

'I'm sure that too is far from true,' Helen reached out a slender, white arm to take her husband's hand. 'And your friendship to my Lord Menelaus is already gift enough.'

'Then come,' Menelaus beamed, 'let us drink to friendship, and be joyful tonight, for tomorrow we will turn our minds to sober things.'

*　　　*　　　*

Paris slept hardly at all that night, and when he did so, it was only to start awake again minutes later. His body was filled with such appetite for life that it balked at every instant lost to consciousness. Such was the agitation of his heart and senses that he found it hard even to keep to his bed, so he wandered out to the balcony of his chamber where the air was heady with the scent of moon-flowers, and a star brighter than the rest — Aphrodite's star — dangled beneath the ripe moon like a jewel. He tried to recall every instant of this first encounter with Helen, every alteration of her face as he spoke to her, or as she became aware of his gaze observing her when the conversation moved elsewhere. He tried to remember every word she had spoken, sounding out each sentence for hidden signs or meanings, but though it exalted his heart simply to think of her at all, again and again he came up against the dispiriting truth that nothing she had said or done gave him a glimmer of hope that she regarded him as anything more than a welcome guest who deserved every courtesy because he was her husband's friend.

Still worse, if he was honest he was forced to admit that Menelaus's uxorious delight in Helen was met, on her side, by a devotion that seemed just as true. Divine Hera had brought this man and woman together in a marriage as unshakeable as Sparta herself, and its calm, ceremonious contentment was ruled by Athena's wisdom as the presiding deity of the city. There appeared to be no room left for Aphrodite's intervention.

Yet somehow Helen must be his. His life depended on it now. Helen *was* his life. Without her beside him, he would wander the world like some hungry shade tormented for ever by the thought of what might have been. The thought was not to be borne. Yet to yearn for the removal of the obstacles that stood between Helen and his desire felt like wishing for the death of a friend. A friend who had freely consented to cleanse his soul of guilt.

And so, as Aeneas slept on untroubled, Paris wandered the night, lurching from hope to despair and back again, finding rest neither inside nor outside himself. At one point, unable to lie on his bed any longer, he left the chamber altogether and walked back through the hall to the intimate room where they had dined that night. He sat where he had sat earlier and gazed across at Helen's chair as though she still reclined there, sipping from the chased silver of her drinking-cup or pushing back a stray lock of her hair. He remembered with what fond admiration she had smiled at Menelaus when Aeneas told the story of the manner in which the Spartan king had saved his life during the boar-hunt in Dardania – a story that she was evidently hearing for the first time. And he winced at the thought of her naked body now lying next to her husband only a few short yards away.

Aware how foolish and impotent the act, he crossed the room to kneel before the chair Helen had occupied at dinner as though some trace of fragrance from her musky perfume might still be discernible there. But there was nothing, only the carved wood and studded leather of the chair and the soft cushions embroidered with figures dancing the spiral dance. His chest felt huge with her absence.

Paris stood up, his mind hot with desperation, reminding himself that he had both a divine commission and the temporal authority of his father to steal the woman away by force if all else failed. This city seemed lax and complacent about its defences. Once out of the citadel there were no gates, no walls. A dash by night to the sea, and Helen was his. It could be done.

In a turmoil of conflicting feelings, he was about to return to his bed when he heard the sound of someone stirring in the hall. His heart leapt to the thought that Aphrodite had acted immediately on his prayer and drawn Helen from her sleep to come to his room. Furtively he moved to a place where he could look out into the hall. What he glimpsed there was not the woman of his dreams but the broad figure of a man in a loose night-robe moving from the chamber door that was just closing behind him to the stairway that led up to the royal apartment. The light of the small oil-lamp he was carrying glistened like bronze off the ruddy gleam of his hair.

The Madness of Aphrodite

For what seemed like hours he had endured the full sunlight of
the courtyard in the sacred precinct as he waited to be admitted
through the great bronze doors of Athena's temple. With Aeneas
at his right and Eteoneus, the king's minister, to his left, Paris
stood barehead and barefoot, wearing a simple white tunic over
a loincloth. Earlier, under the curious gaze of the Spartan crowd,
he had poured libations and offered sacrifices to the goddess at
the stone altar at the foot of the steps before the porch. His fore-
lock had been cut and burned. He had been ritually beaten with
birch branches, then bathed for the third time that day and asperged
with holy water and oils. Now, from inside the temple drifted
the chanted strains of the hymn to the divine one who had
sprung fully armed from the head of Zeus, and was about to pass
judgement on whether or not this stranger in the land could be
cleansed of the pollution he had brought there with him.

Alone of all the people assembled at the temple, Paris knew
that there was more than one occasion on which he had given
offence to Grey-eyed Athena, and that his rejection of her in
favour of Aphrodite on the slopes of Mount Ida might weigh
more heavily with her than did the hapless death of Antheus.
The knowledge filled him with increasing dread.

At last a priest had appeared at the head of the stone steps to summon him inside the temple. Accompanied by his two attendants, and with his head bowed low in respect and abjection, Paris entered the cool shade of the Bronze House of Athena. The priest signalled for Aeneas and Eteoneus to remain by the door as Paris walked in silence between the lines of priests and priestesses, their ministers and choristers, to kneel before the impressive figure of Menelaus who was dressed in the ritual garments of a priest and carried a golden staff. Behind the priest-king stood a tall statue of the goddess, helmeted and wearing the aegis over her snake-robe, with a gorgon-embossed shield over one arm and her long, bronze-tipped spear leaning in the other. As Paris raised his open palm to his brow in the gesture of adoration, the air hung heavy with the swirl of incense about his head.

Menelaus addressed the goddess with solemn words of invocation, then turned to Paris and demanded that he render a truthful account of himself and of the guilt he had incurred through the death of Antheus. When his confession ended with heartfelt words of contrition and a ritual supplication of Athena's mercy, the tunic was unlaced from his shoulders, his hands were bound at his back, and a black hood was pulled down over his head like the sudden thick fall of night. To the plangent sound of music and chanting he was led around the temple until he had lost all sense of direction. He heard a door scrape open, and then he was passing down uneven stone steps where the air felt cold and damp about him. He had not been prepared for any of this. With a searing flash of panic, Paris wondered whether Menelaus had divined his secret intention and meant to do away with him in some dark declivity of this ancient place. His skin was trembling in the chill air.

When the hood was removed he stood blinking in the torch-lit gloom of a rocky cavern somewhere deep inside the hill. By the unstable light, Paris made out flickering, stick-like pictures painted on the stone and, directly ahead of him, the primitive wooden figure of a goddess. She loomed above a charred altar of rough stone with what appeared to be the head of an owl.

The air was acrid with smoke, and the hollow of the cave was suddenly loud with what his stunned heart took for the screaming of a frightened child. Then Menelaus appeared before him, red-haired in the torch-light, no longer dressed in priestly vestments, but wearing what might have been a butcher's leather apron over his naked form. A long blade glinted in his hand.

'Kneel,' he commanded, and when Paris hesitated, staring up at him wide-eyed, Menelaus spoke again above the terrible shrill of screaming. 'Kneel.'

With his hands still tied behind his back, and having no choice now but to pray for the mercy of a goddess whose very face had once been forbidden to the sight of men, Paris did as he was ordered. Words were exchanged in a dialect unknown to him. When he looked up he saw a priest holding a suckling pig by its hind legs in offering. The pale animal shrieked and twisted as it was passed into the grip of Menelaus, then the priest-king lifted its straining body, snout downwards, and drew his knife across its throat. The nerve-splitting squeals fell silent and the hot, bright gush of its life-blood spurted out over Paris's naked head and face and shoulders.

In the taut silence of the cave he could hear Menelaus chanting liturgical words he did not understand. The blood stuck in his hair, it splashed in thick gouts across his eyes and face, and dripped from his jaw to his chest. Tight-lipped, shuddering under the warm, sticky smell of its flow, appalled that so small an animal could hold so much blood, he thought he might choke in that hideous, scarlet shower.

Then it was over. He forced open the clotted lids of his eyes to look through a veil of blood at the ancient figure of the goddess. A priest and priestess at either side of him were pouring water from silver ewers to wash the vivid streaks from his flesh. As the cold streams sluiced about his shoulders, he thought he could feel the pollution of the little boy's death falling from him. But when he gazed up again into the piercing, owl-eyed face of the goddess, he felt like a shrew in her talons. With a certainty that struck to the bottom of his soul he knew there was one offence he had committed which remained so grave in the relentless eyes of Athena that, however long his life-thread might run, that insult to her divine pride would never be forgiven.

Yet he could not bring himself to regret it. He told himself that Aphrodite was there beside him, even in this deep fissure that had been hewn out of the rock at the dawn of time and made sacred to Athena. He stood to be dried, and as the tunic was laced again about his shoulders, Menelaus was smiling across at him, saying, 'The goddess has looked kindly on you, friend.' But there was only one thought pressing at his mind: that it could not be long now before he was back in the fragrance of daylight once again, and in Helen's presence.

A great banquet was held in the palace hall that night. To the applause of the assembled Spartan nobility, not all of whom had been glad to welcome Paris's unclean presence in their city, the Trojan princes presented the gifts they had brought for Menelaus and his queen. These were costly and plentiful, and many had travelled along the spice-roads from lands far to the east and south of the Black Sea. The sheer silks, rare perfumes and finely woven cashmere gowns occasioned much amazement and pleasure, as well as thoughtful remarks on the enviable wealth of Priam's kingdom, and everyone was delighted by a pair of chattering monkeys that were got up in Phrygian robes to look like Paris and Aeneas.

The last gift of all was greeted with wondering gasps of approval when Paris stood behind the queen's chair to fasten at her neck the clasp of a golden chain from which hung a gauzy, intricately worked cascade of jade, lapis and other precious stones. 'I am told that this necklace once adorned a great queen in the east,' he said, 'but were it Aphrodite's *kestos* itself, it would scarcely do justice to the beauty which graces it now.'

'No words of mine could do justice to King Priam's generosity,' Helen blushed with pleasure. 'I thank him for this gift with all my heart.'

Amid the loud exclamations of approval, Paris whispered in
her ear, 'The gift is mine. I offer it in ransom for my heart.'

Before she could catch her breath to reply, he straightened,
smiling at Menelaus, and returned to his chair. The King rose to
express his own delight at the bounty of the gifts. Promising that
his guests would not return empty-handed, he nodded to
Eteoneus, who clapped his hands for the musicians to strike up.
At a beating of drums and gongs a skimpily clad troop of Libyan
tumblers sprang in somersaults and cartwheels across the floor of
the hall.

Paris did not join the loud applause. Turbulent and emotional
after the ordeal of his cleansing, he was still trembling from the
intimacy of the brief contact with Helen's skin. Again and again
he tried to catch her eye, eager to read some sign of response to
his approach, but she was looking studiously elsewhere as she
listened to Aeneas and her husband discussing plans for their
forthcoming mission to Mycenae. Her hands did not finger the
necklace at her breast. Even when a woman approached to admire
its jewels more closely, remarking how finely the jade enhanced
the green fire of her eyes, she gave no indication of anything
more than momentary pleasure. It might have been some trinket
she had bought at a fair.

Paris swigged heavily from his cup. The music clashed in his
head. Fighting an urge to leap onto the table and shout at the
noisy revellers that he was an emissary not just from Troy but
from the goddess Aphrodite herself, he stared as a towering ziggurat
of tumblers mounted upwards to loud applause. He was aware
that the madness of love was making a base ingrate of him, yet
he wanted to threaten these Spartan fools with the fury of the
goddess if they did not immediately rise up and demand that
their king surrender his queen to the arms of the man for whom
fate had always destined her.

The tumblers were replaced by bangled dancing girls, and they
in turn by an Arcadian minstrel who sang first of the hopeless
passion of Echo for Narcissus, and then of Pygmalion's love for

Galatea. So the evening wore on with Paris sighing more than he spoke, and drinking more than he sighed, trying again and again to engage Helen's eyes. When he met only a polite, brief smile or a swiftly withdrawn glance as she turned away to whisper to her husband, Paris found such distant proximity increasingly hard to bear. The fury had long since burned itself out. Overwhelmed by sadness, he got up, making no excuses or apologies, and walked out of the hall to stand alone on a balcony.

He told himself that a kind of madness had possessed him, and there was nothing to be done about it. And though its claims were both too painful and too beautiful to be borne, bear them he must, for the goddess had offered him love and he had chosen to accept the gift. He had wished this fate on himself, and all the rites that went with it, and not for a single moment did he regret that choice – though it now seemed that it opened a need in his heart that could never be requited. But if that was the price of the exaltation he had felt on looking into Helen's eyes, then he was content to pay it. And if he was forbidden to savour the joys of love with her, then he would savour the pain.

After a time he heard a quiet cough at his back. When he turned, Eteoneus was standing there saying, 'My lord, the king is concerned lest our Spartan entertainment is not to your taste.'

'Not at all, not at all,' Paris answered dismally. 'The wine is strong. I needed to take the air. Tell the king that I will shortly return to his side.' But he had no heart for it. Minutes later, he was still staring across the river at the misty plain when he heard the soft notes of Helen's voice at his back. 'If you will not come of your own accord,' she said, 'my Lord Menelaus bids me come to fetch you.'

'Because no man in his right mind would refuse to do your bidding?' he said hoarsely, the blood beating in his throat.

Helen flushed a little and glanced away to collect herself. 'Because he misses your company, and fears that the ordeals of the day may have proved too much for you.'

Staring intently into her troubled eyes, he said, 'The ordeals of the day were as nothing compared to the ordeal of this night.'

Helen took a step back as though at a suddenly opened furnace door.

'Has someone displeased you?' she asked.

'You,' he accused her softly. 'You have displeased me.'

She stood before him, her chin tilted, her cheeks flushed as though he had struck her. Yet her voice was steady as she said, 'My lord?'

'I know you heard me when I clasped this bauble about your neck,' he hissed, 'yet you refuse me an answer.'

Angered by his abandonment of all discretion, she withstood his gaze. 'You are my husband's friend and I can refuse you nothing that honour permits. Sir, I thank you for this exquisite gift, which I cannot now accept.' But when she made to unfasten the clasp at her neck, he reached out to prevent her.

'Keep it, I beg you,' he said. 'Forgive me. I am not in my right mind.'

Her throat was dry, her alarmed heart knocking at her chest. Helen glanced quickly about to see if her turmoil was observed. Then she turned her slender body askance to him. 'I think you must be exhausted from the day,' she said. 'Shall I tell my husband that your need is to retire?'

'Tell him that you have looked on a man who is sickening with love for you. Tell him that the man may not have long to live unless that love is returned. Tell him that you have become a stranger to your former self and that his every glance now commands the entire attention of your soul. Tell him,' he added, urgently catching her wrist as she turned away, 'that when a god summons us it is madness to refuse.'

She stood, collecting her wits, her face flushed, eyes bright with the exaltation of her fear. 'Is Prince Paris so deluded that he thinks he is a god?'

'No. But I serve one, lady. And she is powerful.'

He heard her breath catch in her throat. He thought he saw a sudden hectic commotion of excitement in her eyes.

She said, 'If you do not release my hand, I will cry out that there is a traitor in my husband's house, one whose thankless heart is utterly unworthy of the kindness and friendship he has been shown.'

He found it intolerable that she should think of him so.

'And if I do?' he said.

Her eyes were turned away. 'We will forget this. We will think no more of it. We will try once more to be friends, you and I.'

Paris tightened his grip a moment longer before saying, 'I cannot promise so much. Say what you like to your husband. My life is in the hand I give back to you now – but it was already there, long before I came to Sparta. Crush it or set it free to love you. Either way, its desire for you will not be extinguished.'

Helen's lips were parted. She held the wrist he had gripped, tenderly, as though his touch had bruised it. Nothing in the world was quite behaving as it should. Even the lamp in the sconce by the door was smoking.

Then she shook her head and turned back into the hall.

Paris followed her scent through the din of revelry, watching the sway of her back, triumphing at least in the knowledge that she would sleep no better than he that night. They found Menelaus and Aeneas laughing together with a tawny-haired woman whose breasts hung loosely as she leaned over them to pour more wine. Raising his cup, the king beamed up at his wife. 'What did I tell you, Aeneas?' he cried. 'Helen's beauty is like a lodestone. It draws all manner of men along with it, whether they will or no. Paris, we have lacked your company. Come, take more wine with us. Or is it true what Eteoneus says – that you're finding Aphrodite's milk too strong for your head?'

'It will be the first time,' Aeneas laughed. 'There have been many nights when he's drunk me under the table.'

'But this has been a strange and powerful day,' Paris frowned.

'True,' Menelaus conceded. Already drunk, he was brimming with affectionate concern. 'Yet the shadow has passed from you now. We washed it away in the Bronze House of Athena. Be merry, my friend.'

Before Paris could find an answer, Helen spoke in a firm voice. 'Prince Paris is weary, husband, and not yet wholly himself. There will be other nights for merriment, but I think that now his need is for sleep.'

Menelaus made a gesture of disappointment. Blearily he studied Paris's pallid face. Always a straightforward man, he was sometimes puzzled by the turbid shifts of emotion in his Asian friends. Then a thought occurred to him. He grinned up at Paris, gesturing with his cup. 'Cast your eyes about the room,' he demanded. 'There must be some woman here whom you would like to warm your bed tonight?'

'Were things otherwise . . .' Paris answered, hoarsely apologetic. 'But your lady wife is as wise as she is beautiful. I believe she reads my mind aright.'

Disappointed, Menelaus shrugged, and made a wry face at Aeneas, who was frowning at his side, perplexed by his friend's unusual demeanour. The Spartan king swayed a little as he got to his feet. 'Sleep if you must,' he said. 'But tomorrow – Aeneas and I have been making plans. Tomorrow we go hunting. We will camp out in the mountains together.' He closed his arms round Paris and warmly patted his back. 'A night or two of wild air will bring you back to yourself. Let's see if we can't find another she-bear to suckle you!' Menelaus was laughing at his jest when he caught his wife's eye. 'Dream well, friend,' he said more quietly. 'The Furies are gone. Your soul is cleansed. You are free to live your life as you wish once more.'

Paris was woken from heavy sleep late the next morning by a rough shaking of his shoulder. 'What's the matter with you, man?' Aeneas was saying. 'You were moaning in your sleep last night, and now with the morning half-over you're still lying here like a drunkard in the street. Menelaus is waiting for us. He's eager for the hunt. Rouse yourself or you'll offend our host.'

Paris dragged himself up from the bed with his head between his hands.

When Aeneas pulled back the drapes, fierce sunlight splintered at his fingers. Paris lifted a haggard face to his friend.

'You look like a gorgon's head!' Aeneas frowned. 'Are you sick or what?'

For a reckless moment Paris was about to confide in him, but he shook his head to clear it and saw that the time was not right. Aeneas was too frank and candid a soul. He was too close in his friendship to Menelaus and would not be able to conceal his trepidation if he knew what desperate plan was on his friend's mind. And if Paris failed to keep his own feelings under control, the King of Sparta would scent trouble soon enough.

'I don't know,' he groaned. 'My head is ringing like a gong.'

'There's a wench I know with a pitcher of water to pour over it. Come on, Paris, shape yourself. Menelaus was too gracious to comment on your behaviour last night, but I heard others remark on it – until Helen took you under her wing, that is. But the king means to hunt today and we're both eager to leave. Can I tell him you'll be ready within the hour?'

Eyes closed under the hand at his brow, Paris nodded. 'Give me time to wash and make my offering to Aphrodite,' he muttered, 'and I'll be with you.'

But when he came down to the hall he found a tumult of confusion there.

The air outside shook to the barking of dogs as they snapped and whined together, impatient for the chase, but a group of old women with faces gnarled as walnuts were moaning and keening in the hall and beating their breasts. Slaves were bustling trunks out to a wagon. Outside in the courtyard, farriers were backing a sprightly team of horses up to the yoke of Menelaus's chariot. The king himself stood in hurried council with Eteoneus and his other ministers, while Helen looked on, pale with anxiety, clutching her frightened daughter Hermione in her arms.

Aeneas crossed the hall to meet Paris at the foot of the stair. 'It seems we've picked a bad time to come,' he said. 'A messenger from Agamemnon has just informed Menelaus that King Catreus has died. He has to leave at once.'

'King Catreus?'

'He's their grandfather on their mother's side. A Cretan. His funeral rites must take place soon, so they have to sail for Crete tonight. The whole palace is in disarray.'

'What about Helen?' Paris demanded.

'Helen?' Aeneas seemed surprised by the question. 'What about her?'

'Will she go to Crete? Is she going with him?'

'I don't know.' Aeneas frowned. 'I'm not sure if it's been decided yet.'

Drawn by the sudden howling of the child, Paris turned to look back across the hall where he saw Helen in urgent consultation with Menelaus. She handed her wailing daughter to a serving-woman for comfort but the child was kicking and shrieking as the woman carried her away. Helen turned back to her distracted husband, evidently entreating him.

'We should offer our condolences,' Paris said.

Aeneas reached out to stop him. 'In good time,' he said. 'Can't you see the king has his hands full right now? He'll speak to us before he goes.'

So Paris had to wait and watch while, through constant interruption from his counsellors and stewards, Menelaus spoke softly to Helen, holding her by the arms and brushing a tear from her cheek with his thumb. Eventually he embraced her, looking about the hall as he did so until his eyes fell on his Trojan friends. With his arm about his wife, he crossed the marble floor to join them. 'Forgive me, friends, but grievous circumstances call me away.'

'We've been told of your loss,' Aeneas said, 'and our grief goes with you. It's clear you have much to attend to. Please don't concern yourself about us. We shall shortly make our own preparations for departure.'

'By no means,' Menelaus demurred. 'I shall return within the week and will bring Agamemnon back to Sparta with me. Then we can give our minds to what most concerns us at this time. In the meantime, Eteoneus will see to all your needs, and I have asked my queen to show you royal entertainment. I cannot hunt today, alas, but you certainly must. Listen – the dogs insist on it.'

He glanced, smiling, at Paris's pallid face. 'If you have the head for it, that is! What is mine is yours. Make free of my home till my return.'

'May your gods go with you,' Paris said, 'and give you comfort in your loss.'

Menelaus nodded, clapped a hand about the shoulder of each man, and turned to Helen, who glanced up at him in dismay. 'Be of good heart,' he said. 'I entrust my friends to you. Honour them as you would myself.' Then, after making a few last arrangements with his ministers, he was gone.

Was Aphrodite so ruthless in pursuit of her ends, Paris wondered, that she was prepared to kill off an old man so that a young man's heart might thrive? Perhaps it was so. Perhaps King Catreus had long been ready for the grave.

But what mortal understood the workings of a god? The only certain thing was that Menelaus was far from his palace now and his wife had said nothing to arouse his suspicion.

Paris feigned sick that day. He told Aeneas that he had no stomach for the hunt, but the day was clear, the pack baying to be freed, and the huntsmen ready, so Aeneas must certainly go. 'I know you're eager to discover what game these Spartan mountains hold. And I'll be well by the time you get back. Bring me a bearskin to amuse Menelaus!'

After Aeneas had left, Paris remained in his chamber for an hour that seemed endless before going down to look for her. Helen was nowhere to be found. He came across the place where the women of the house worked at their looms and spindles but he could see her nowhere among them, and the women giggled so much at his unexpected arrival in the weaving hall that he quickly withdrew. Nor was she walking in the gardens of the palace, or visible anywhere among the streets of the market-place.

By mid-afternoon, when the halls of the palace had fallen quiet in the heat of the day, he decided to risk entering the private rooms of the royal apartment.

He found the principal receiving room with its tall throne empty. A glance into a side chamber along the passage showed a plump serving-woman snoozing on a couch with the child Hermione in a cot beside her clutching a rag doll in one hand and sucking the thumb of the other as she slept. He pulled quietly away. The studded door to the next room was securely locked – Paris guessed that the king's treasury was here, or an armoury perhaps. Knowing that he must now be approaching the royal bedroom, he stole along the corridor scarcely able to breathe, and came to a trembling halt before the bronze-bound double door. He knew there was no excuse he could make if someone other than Helen was in there, sweeping the floor or changing the linen on the bed. But it seemed improbable at this hour and he could hear no sound through the door, so he threw the latch. It clattered in the still air. The doors swung open and he was looking into an airy chamber filled with light from a balcony that looked across the gardens to the river and the mountains far beyond. A huge bed built of cedar-wood, inlaid with gold and ivory, and with a pair of leopards carved at its head, looked towards the balcony. It was covered with plump pillows and gorgeously woven throws. A wooden chest stood at its foot. On the wall above the bed-head hung a tapestry of the Three Graces dancing together in a meadow of asphodels and violets. The other walls were painted in carmine, blue and gold. Against one of them, the iridescent hues of a peacock-feather fan shimmered in the breeze from the open window.

This was where she slept and dreamed. This was where her

husband made love to her each night. He had expected to be tormented by the thought, but he was now so certain of the invincibility of his own claim to Helen that he remained unruffled by it. Menelaus might have lain with Helen, and even sired a child on her. But the woman in his bed was not the real Helen of Sparta because Helen herself did not yet know who she truly was. How could she when the secret of her true life was known only to the goddess and himself?

Paris crossed the room to where a pair of inner doors opened on two separate closets, one of which was Helen's dressing-room. He could smell her perfume on the air. Many garments hung in racks there. He took the soft material of the nearest in both hands and clutched it to his face. Then he crossed to the table where her rich collection of cosmetics was assembled with the brushes, powder-puffs, files and combs neatly ranged beside them. There were posset-boxes made of sandalwood and many small apothecaries' flasks. Several caskets opened to reveal a small treasury of rings and bracelets, necklaces and earrings, finely worked armbands, brooches, diadems, jewelled hair-nets, clasps and fastening-pins. He looked for, but could not find, the jade necklace that was his token to her. Had she cast it aside, or put it somewhere secret for safe-keeping? But then his eyes fell on the silver scent-flask figured in the shape of Aphrodite holding a dove that Helen had prized among the other gifts he brought.

Clearing a space on the dressing-table, he lifted down the polished bronze plaque framed with dolphins that was her mirror, and laid it there. Then he took the stopper from the spout of the flask and in a thin drizzle of the perfume tried to write *I love you* across the face of the mirror, but the letters refused to keep their shape and began to evaporate on the air. Looking about he found a pot of the paint with which she must darken the lashes of her eyes. He took a brush, wetted it on his tongue, and began to write. The words were crudely done, and he had no time to worry, as he licked the brush again and again, whether or not the paint was poisonous. If it was, so be it: at least his message would survive him. And even his failure with the perfume proved a kind of success, for he had used so much of the costly stuff that the atmosphere of the closet had changed. It no longer smelled of Sparta, but of Troy.

When he opened the double doors of the bed-chamber to let himself out he heard the child whimpering in the nursery, a small noise but loud enough to wake her nurse. Furtively he slipped along the passage, peered through the hinge-crack of the half-open door and saw the nurse stooping to lift Hermione from her cot. She was tutting and shushing as she did so. Paris slipped quickly past the door and on to the end of the passage. He had just reached the foot of the stairs and was about to step out into the garden when a male voice behind him said, 'Was there something you wanted?'

Startled, Paris turned and saw Eteoneus frowning at him from the doorway that led to the kitchen quarters at the end of the hall.

'I was just . . .' Paris found the easy smile with which he had so often charmed the world, 'I was wondering where I might find the Lady Helen.'

'My lady understood that you were ill,' Eteoneus answered. 'She left instructions that you were to be visited every two hours if you did not appear. Her wise-woman Polydamna has been given care of you. She knocked at your door earlier. As there was no answer, she assumed you were asleep.'

Paris was on the point of agreeing that must have been the case, when he remembered he had been seen walking the streets. 'I was feeling better and thought I would take the air,' he said instead. 'That must have been when the woman knocked.' He smiled again. 'Tell me, where can I find her?'

'Polydamna is in the women's quarters. Shall I have her called?'

'I meant the Lady Helen.'

'Ah! My lady is at her devotions. She is making offerings for King Catreus, whom she greatly mourns. She would not wish to be disturbed.'

'And doubtless she prays for her husband's safe return?'

Eteoneus nodded, wondering a little at this puzzling Trojan's smile.

'I understand. Then I must patiently wait on her pleasure.' Paris glanced out into the bright sunlight. 'In the garden perhaps. I see there is a shrine to Aphrodite there. I too have devotions to make.'

With a courteous nod he turned away and walked across the pillared terrace into the garden. The grapes were fattening on the vine-trellis, and cypresses and tall plane trees shaded his way through oleanders and hibiscus to the distant myrtle grove where Aphrodite had her shrine. Entering the grove, Paris smiled at the statue of Priapus, a bearded, misshapen figure carved from fig-wood, who stood with his left hand resting on one hip, while his right hand held a flask of oil from which he anointed his impressively swollen member. Someone – a hopeful amorist presumably – had left an offering of pomegranates and quinces there. A blackbird chattered at Paris's approach. Then he was through into the sacred precinct of the goddess.

For a long time he knelt in silent meditative prayer where the small marble statue of Aphrodite overlooked a spring pouring from the rocks. The goddess stood on a plinth, dressing her hair amid the sharp, sweet scent of deep pink damask roses. Above her head, doves flapped loud wings from tree to tree across the glade or basked in sunlight murmuring. Somewhere in the distance a donkey sawed and wheezed its complaint against its load. But Paris was listening for Aphrodite to whisper encouragement and counsel in his ear.

After a time he got up to sit on the bench in a sheltered arbour woven from sweet-smelling myrtle switches. The sensuality of the place, the stillness of its scented air, the sound of water in the heat of the afternoon, everything conspired to fuel the desire for Helen that was aching through all his limbs. His prayer became a magical incantation. He was summoning her now.

But it was a child's voice that came to him through the trees, the voice of a little girl: Hermione! If Helen was walking her daughter through the garden it was unlikely she would bring the child here. Paris got to his feet. After a moment's hesitation he walked swiftly out of the grove, past the Priapus, in the direction where he could hear the child prattling.

He came out between two bay trees and saw Hermione romping in a patch of sunlight as she threw a ball to the fat nurse who stood across the grass from her. 'Catch it, Chryse,' she was calling, 'you have to catch it.' But the ball fell short. Sighing, the nurse bent to pick it up and when she threw it back, it came too high, passed between the child's raised hands, bounced once, and then rolled across the grass to where Paris stood in dense shade. With her eyes fixed on the ball, Hermione came running his way, calling back over her shoulder, and noticed him only when he stooped to pick up the ball. Laughing, he made to throw it gently back to her, but the child had come to a shocked halt, and was staring up at him as though a ghost was standing there.

'Catch,' he invited, bending a little, gesturing with the ball.

The child's face shrank with fear. She brought both clenched hands up to her mouth and let out a frightened cry. Dismayed by the response, he took a step towards her, but Hermione turned on her heels and ran back across the grass towards the nurse, crying out, 'Save me, Chryse, save me from the foreign man!' Then she threw her thin arms around the hips of the nurse. The woman put a hand down to the little girl's head where it was now buried in her skirts, and said, 'What's the matter with you, child?' Hermione raised her face briefly to glance back where Paris looked awkwardly on, and he was horrified to hear the child whimper. 'It's the man who kills children. I want my daddy, I want my daddy,' before she burst into a noisy torrent of tears.

The nurse looked up at the foreigner in dismay, made the sign to ward off the evil eye, then picked up the squalling child and hurried away.

Paris was left shaken in the garden's shattered peace.

★   ★   ★

He was still there half an hour later, utterly downcast by a chain of thought that had begun with the realization that for Helen to have a child was a far more complex matter than he had calculated, and all the more so as the child seemed possessed by an irrational fear of him.

He went back into the myrtle grove to contemplate his problem, but apart from the infant Eros, who was of quite a different order, he saw that Aphrodite had as little to do with children as she did with morality. She was the single-minded goddess of sexual passion and desire. Her duties ended where conception began. What possible help could she be against a hostile child?

Yet he found it impossible to believe that Aphrodite had brought him here and spirited Menelaus so swiftly away without some larger plan in mind. The alternative – that after such an auspicious start, a tearful five year old should stand as an insuperable obstacle between himself and Helen – was a torment too bitter to contemplate. Surely he had charm enough to win the child round?

He was considering how best to set about this when he heard the sound of someone approaching through the garden. Expecting Eteoneus to come with a disapproving frown across his face, Paris leapt to his feet from where he sat in the arbour and saw Helen striding across the grass towards him. Her face was flushed, her hair in disarray. His first exclamation of surprise turned into a wondering smile, but she had reached him before he could speak, was lifting her hand, and then she smacked him hard across the face with all the strength she could command. Paris stood, blinking back the tears that jumped from him, shaking his dazed head. The skin of his cheek smarted like fire.

Startled by the crack of skin against skin, a flight of doves were scattering their bright wings about the grove.

'How dare you?' she was gasping. 'How dare you?'

Against the ringing in his ears he said, 'I'm sorry, I'm so sorry. I didn't mean to frighten the child.'

She stared at him as though his mind was impaired. Her eyes

were flashing the fiercest glitter of sea-blue-green that he had ever seen outside a sunlit tempest off the Dardanian coast. He was trying to say that the child must have overheard something about him and misunderstood, but Helen erased his words with a furious gesture of her open palms across the air. 'To go into our private rooms, to finger my things, to leave the spoor of your absurd message for any chambermaid to smell! How could you? How dare you?'

Before he could stop her, she cracked her hand across his cheek again.

He pulled back, raising his arms to defend himself from further attack, and then he was laughing, laughing out loud through the sting of pain as he fell back onto the bench under the myrtle boughs.

She stared at him, appalled by his laughter, more beside herself with anger than at any time in her life before. 'If you ever dare to do such a thing again,' she hissed, 'I will stab you with my knife.'

The laughter stopped. They were both panting as they stared at each other across the trembling space between.

'Then do it.' Paris raised his open hands exposing his unde-fended chest. 'Bring your knife and kill me now, for if you will not love me I'm already a dead man.'

Her hands were both gripped tight — tight as knots, tight enough to hurt — as though only so could she restrain a fury that had already made her a stranger to herself and was now threatening to drag her, like the muscular currents of a flood, into a chaos beyond recall. If there had been a knife to hand in that moment she would certainly have used it.

As it was, all she could do was gasp — as much to herself as to the deranging man across from her — 'I would do it, I will do it.'

Again, after a shocked moment in which he realized that she was speaking her truth, he laughed.

Staring at him in incredulous rage, she said, 'I think you must be mad.'

'Believe me,' he answered at once, 'there is nothing I will not say or do to make you love me. If that is madness then, yes, I am mad.'

Helen pulled her body to its full height. Her heart was a mallet pounding her, strike by strike, like a stake into the ground where she was making her stand. 'I am Helen, Queen of Sparta,' she said, 'not some easy chit of a Trojan girl to lure into your bed. Do you believe I could ever love a man despicable enough to betray his friend while his back was turned?'

'Yes,' he hissed. And again, 'yes.'

'A man who would feign sickness and tell lies and steal about my house like a common thief.'

'Yes.'

'Then as well as a madman, you're a fool.'

'Then let it be so,' he said. 'But if I am mad, then I'm mad for love. If I'm a fool, I am a fool for love.'

Somewhere in the myrtle boughs around them, a dove clattered its wings.

She stood, trembling under the entreaty of his eyes. Knowing that he was gone beyond all reason and that if she remained longer in that glade she too might lose all dignity and control, she said, 'It would be best if you went from Sparta. But you are my husband's guest, not mine.' She heard her voice shaking as she added, 'If you choose to stay, do not expect to find me here.'

Helen drew in her breath and turned to walk away. But she had taken only three strides when he called, 'Why did you not tell him what passed between us last night?'

Had she walked on, a world might have been saved; but she stopped, and the accusation in his question caught her by the ankle like a hobbling rope.

She turned again to face him, fiery-eyed, 'Because you are his friend,' she said. 'Because Menelaus loves you and it would break his heart.'

'Yes—' he held her stare unflinching '—it will break his heart.'

For a time there was only the sound of water pouring between the rocks.

When he saw that she had not moved, Paris sat down on the bench in the myrtle arbour. Like a man suddenly exhausted, he rested his elbows on his knees and held his head between his hands. Hoarsely he said, 'It is the madness of Aphrodite. Lady, I have loved you since long before I came to Sparta. It is for love of you I came.'

She heard him at last. She heard the finality of his utterance. She heard its truth. But her will was protesting still. Bewildered, she reached for reason. 'How could you love me? You hadn't even seen me. You didn't know me. It's not me you loved but some fantastic dream inside your head.'

'You were the dream inside my head. The goddess put you there, and when she first whispered your name to me I knew you for my fate. The heart knows such things. And now that I've met you it's no longer a dream.'

For a moment she was held there, gripped by his eyes. She knew that it was imperative to turn now and walk away. She turned.

He whispered. 'Lady, you have been promised to me since the dawn of time. A whole world is turning on this moment.'

Her back was to him, and when she spoke, her voice was barely more than a murmur, as though it did not matter whether he heard or not. 'My world is here. I belong here, with the husband I love.'

He nodded, smiling as though in sympathy. 'I have watched you together and for a time I thought the love between you was such that the goddess must have misled me. Yet you have shown me otherwise.'

She rounded on him. 'How so?'

'Because there was more passion in the blows you gave me than ever you showed him. That was why I laughed — not to mock you, or out of crazy folly, but for the simple joy of knowing that you would never have struck me like that if I did not trouble your soul. I think you know me, lady. I think you knew me from the first moment we looked at each other. I think that you have begun to feel the madness of the goddess too.'

He had got up from the bench as he was speaking and taken two steps towards her. Helen backed away at his approach, but she had seen that what she had thought was arrogance might simply be a certainty so clear that it might be taken for a form of innocence.

'If there was passion there,' she said, 'it was no more than righteous anger. You have no right to invade my life like this.'

He said quietly, 'And if that life is finished? You can't go back to it now, not as it was. Menelaus is gone and there is no safety. Look for it again with him, and you will find only a tedium of years in which to wonder what might have happened if you had responded when the goddess called. There is a new life waiting for you. The life you have kept in hiding. Be brave and let it be.'

The terror of the words he uttered, the scent from the damask roses and the myrtle boughs, the narcotic whirr of the crickets in the heat of the afternoon, and the splash of water breaking from the rock – all these swirled inside her like the presence of a god. Helen turned her gaze to look where Aphrodite shamelessly dressed her hair, bare-breasted, the folds of her gown fallen about her hips, careless of everything but the sensual pulse of life delivered over into love. How many times had she studied that statue, restlessly aware that life must have more to offer than the repeated ceremonies of her daily round, the comforts of an undemanding role, and the easy sigh of satisfaction with which Menelaus consummated each swift and grateful act of love? But she had revered chaste Artemis when she was a girl, and now, as wife and queen, she honoured Hera and Athena. She told herself that it was better to choose Hera's bounteous ears of wheat, or Athena's loaded olive-trees, over the thorny roses of the Golden One. Better to resist the claims of passion than be swept away as its victim. Yet it was she who had placed this statue here.

And he was dismantling the world around her.

Helen shook her head. What was this mad Trojan asking of her? Could he really imagine that she would put all her life at risk for the sake of his devastating smile and these extravagant professions of immortal love? Was he anything more than a younger, more personable brigand of the flesh than Theseus had been – yet without that great king's glory? She recalled that day again – the heart-stopping terror of it, yes, but also the surge of exhilaration with which she had imagined herself carried off by a god in the moments before she came to her senses and saw an old man lusting over her.

'Such beauty must be less a blessing than a curse,' Theseus had murmured, and the words had pushed her soul so far into hiding that it remained beyond the reach of even her husband's considerate hand. Could this man really have fathomed those depths and seen it cowering there? Did he truly know how to call it forth? Why else, despite herself, was she trembling at his words?

And at the touch, tender and undemanding, of his hands at her shoulders?

His face was pressing softly into the hair at the nape of her neck. She could feel the stir of his breath. 'I know you have not yet had time to learn to love me,' he was whispering. 'But you can. You will.'

She pulled away. 'Hear me,' she said again, 'I love my husband. I have a husband who loves me. A husband who loves me dearly.'

He considered for a moment before saying what came into his mind. Then he uttered it quietly.

'A husband who steals from your chamber to another in the night.'

Her eyes widened, her nostrils flared.

'How can you know that?'

'Because I saw it with my own eyes. I came down on that first night to where we had dined together. I couldn't sleep for thinking of you. I saw him then.'

Drawing in her breath, she lifted her chin. 'Menelaus is king here. He has a king's rights.'

'What rights could possibly take him from your bed?'

'His right to a son,' Helen said, 'which is a thing I cannot give him.'

Paris stood winded by her answer.

With a kind of defiance the words burst from her. 'So yours is a barren dream, you see. A barren dream of a barren woman.' But before she looked away he saw the anguish in her face, and his heart went out to her. For a time their two vulnerable lives confronted one another across the still glade.

'I am so sorry,' he whispered.

And she looked up into a face so softened by compassion that she might have wept.

Who was this man? He had the appearance of a prince but there was such clear, uncourtly candour in his gaze that he might have been a country swain. So perhaps he was, simply, what he so passionately claimed to be — a man so far in love with her that he understood nothing else.

Unable to speak, to move, she was thinking, 'If my death is here then the goddess has sent it.'

But it was of life he was speaking — a life in which they might come to share the passion of the gods. A life such as only those elected into love could know, and of them only those who were prepared to offer everything.

He had reached out, tenderly, to touch her again. Immediately she pulled away as if she had opened her eyes to find herself on a chasm's edge and was reaching back for the safety of everything she knew. Though he had come no closer, she stretched out a hand in refusal, keeping him at a distance, repeating the word 'No' four or five times like a protective charm.

Gently, he shook his head. 'I think we are in the hands of the goddess now.' He reached out to pluck a damask rose from the bush. 'She means well by us.' He pricked the pad of one of his fingers on a thorn, and then pressed it softly to her lips till they too were smudged with blood.

Helen took another step away, open-mouthed. 'Do you blame the goddess for all the havoc that you wreak?'

Paris smiled down at her with the serene calm of a true believer. 'No.' Gravely he shook his head. 'I praise her.'

171

Moving closer again, he threaded the green stem through the tied-back tresses of her hair. 'I shall wait for you tonight,' he whispered. 'If you can deny what I have said, then leave me to pine alone and condemn us both to wither unrequited. Otherwise come to me.' Then he brushed past her shoulder and walked from the myrtle grove without a backward glance.

The Flight from Sparta

Aeneas's ship, the *Gorgona,* was the first to make landfall in Troy. The voyage home had proved less placid than the voyage out as a stiff gale blew up, forcing the ship to make way through rain against a heavy swell. Nor was the mood of Aeneas less turbulent than that of the sea he crossed. Already furious with Paris, he was convinced that his love-crazed friend had deliberately altered course in the dark of the storm to shake him off. So for days the *Gorgona* had battled the dirty weather alone, charting a course through the Cyclades, expecting at any moment to see an Argive warship overhauling them out of the dark horizon.

The odds were all against it, of course, for the Trojans would have been well out into the eastern sea before the news reached Menelaus in Crete. Yet the normally equable disposition of the Dardanian prince was so overwrought by his friend's treacherous behaviour that he lived in daily expectation of divine retribution. His crew, many of whom had grumbled at the hasty departure in foul weather from a port they had come to like, were already murmuring that Hera must have sent this storm against them.

Aeneas was not surprised, therefore, to find no sign of the *Aphrodite* in the waters of the Hellespont. In fact, as he muttered blackly to his sailing-master, he would have wagered all Dardania against a mouldy fig that if Paris's vessel was still afloat, it was laid up in some convenient bay while he cooed and dandled with the woman for whom he had put everything at risk.

As soon as he was ashore Aeneas hastened to his father's palace at the foot of Mount Ida to report on the disastrous outcome of the mission. Anchises listened, impassive as marble, from behind unseeing eyes as his son tried to make sense of Paris's insane behaviour.

'I blame myself for not having read the signs earlier. When I had half a chance to think about it afterwards, they seemed obvious enough. His manner at the banquet was so distracted that he came close to giving offence to our hosts.

'And I've never known him to be ill before – not even when he was drinking far into the night and tupping the palace-women like a randy ass. Yet two days after we arrived, there he was, complaining of sickness and headaches, and lying in bed when there was good hunting to be done. I put it down to the rigours of the cleansing ordeal at the time, but he's seen more than enough blood not to quail at the smell of it. He should have felt freed by the purgation, uplifted by it even. If I hadn't been so eager for the hunt myself, I might have suspected something dubious was happening when he hurried me off to the moun-tains as soon as the king's back was turned. I should have seen that . . .' Aeneas halted the rush of self-recriminatory thought. 'But he must have been so far out of his senses by then that I doubt I could have stopped him.'

'Not *out* of his senses,' Anchises said. 'Intoxicated by them. I recognized it in that youth a long time ago. His adoration of Aphrodite was always excessive. I tried to counsel him once in the wisdom of Apollo. But who was I to berate him for his love of the Golden One, when I have blighted my own life in her service?' Sighing, the old king pulled his cloak closer about his shoulders. 'Do not rebuke yourself. Aphrodite was always single-minded in her obsessions. If she has chosen Paris for the instrument of her passion, then nothing you or I or anyone could do would keep him from his fate.'

'But Menelaus was his friend,' Aeneas protested. 'The man even saved my life! And now I'm left torn between them. Zeus knows, I've always loved Paris – ever since that first day when I watched him bloody Deiphobus's nose. But I feel his treachery could scarcely be greater if it was *my* wife he had stolen.'

'Be thankful, therefore, that Helen was not your wife, for Aphrodite would not have spared you that betrayal.' Anchises's sigh was heavy with resignation. 'In any case, Paris has betrayed us all. You and he went to Sparta in search of peace. What he has done provides the Argives with a perfect case for war.'

'Unless someone more powerful than me can persuade him to give her up.'

'Do you think he will ever do that?'

Aeneas thought for only a moment before shaking his head again. 'No. He is gone beyond all reason. I don't believe he will.'

'But what of Helen?' Anchises said. 'Might she be persuaded to return?'

'Who can say what a woman might do in her circumstances? I tried to speak to her, I warned her of the consequences of her actions, but she was like a woman in a dream . . . except that there was a gleam in her eye such as I have seen only in the green stare of a wolf that knows it may die but will go down to the end enduring all.' Aeneas drew in his breath deeply. 'I think that Helen too must be possessed by a god. How else could she have let herself abandon her child?'

'She left her children in Sparta?'

'She has only one. A daughter, Hermione, a child almost as beautiful as Helen herself. For some reason – a prophetic instinct perhaps – the child had taken against Paris. And in the end Helen saw she must choose between Paris and her daughter. Had they tried to take Hermione with them, the child would have made the night loud with her screams. They could never have left the palace unseen.'

'Did you not challenge Helen on this score?'

'Of course I did! She answered that Hermione had always been her father's child, and that it would be more cruel to take her than to leave her behind. Whether she believed this or not, I cannot say. Certainly she is already suffering for the choice she made.'

'Passion always exacts a price. Paris will come to pay it in his time. But we must do what we can to make sure that all Troy is not made to answer for his crime.' Aeneas turned his blind gaze on his son and reached out a hand to draw him closer. 'We will speak with Antenor first – he has Priam's ear and is no friend to Paris. Then the three of us together will confront the High King with this news. It cannot be long before the sons of Atreus are hammering at his door.'

'And all Argos has sworn to defend Menelaus's right to Helen.'

'Yes,' Anchises sighed. 'I begin to fear that a still greater power than Aphrodite lies behind these events. If Sky-Father Zeus has decided that the time has come to cut a swathe through mortal men, then war might prove terrible indeed. We Dardanians must consider carefully how much we are prepared to risk for Troy.'

And what of the lovers meanwhile? Once they had found their way into each other's arms, they would have sequestered themselves away for many days in an uninterrupted dream of love if they had been left free to choose; for in the few hours they were able to spend together that first night they were like astonished travellers entering a realm of the senses such as neither had known before. All trace of hostility between them had instantly dissolved, transformed by some subtle alchemy of love into a tender ferocity of desire to know the other more deeply in every crevice of their being, every gesture of feeling and of thought. And when the love-making was done, they lay side by side, talking and talking about their lives, as though their souls had always been intimate, though separated by the world for many years.

Gazing into Helen's eyes, Paris recalled how an ascetic priest visiting Troy out of India had once tried to persuade him that the human soul journeys through many lifetimes in search of peace. Though he had laughed off this philosophy as extravagant at the time, it now seemed easy to believe that he and Helen had known each other long before they met, in some other time, some other world. He whispered this into her ear as he lay beside her, and she smiled at him, saying, 'Perhaps it was in another life that I gave you that mark about your neck – unless some other woman has already set her teeth in you!'

'I remember nothing of any other woman,' he whispered. 'If there were any, they were only the vaguest dreams of you. But that mark has been with me from birth. My mother said it was as though I had been bitten by passion, and I swear I have never known true passion before. Perhaps you are right and Aphrodite left that sign for you to know me by. Come, let me lift your hair and brand you with the same mark, so we will know each other again in all the lives to come.'

'I believe I would know you,' she said as he raised his mouth from her, 'if I were deaf and blind, and an age of men had passed between this life and the next.'

'And I you,' he replied, 'if the sun were to die and there was only endless night.'

Yet at other moments, as they gazed into the unfathomable wonder of each other's eyes, the sense of accomplished union was so complete that there was no need for speculation – or of any words at all – to comprehend what was happening between them: the whole universe was simply and entirely love.

Yet if there were times when their hearts stood still that night, time itself would have no stop, and long before the first cock crowed, alarm was gathering in Helen's heart. Despite her lover's pleas and protests, she dragged herself from the bed just before dawn and hurried back to the royal apartment, fearful at every turn that she might be seen. Alone in her marriage bed, she shook at the knowledge of what had been done and what was now asked of her. Her mind refused all thought. She stared into the gathering light, knowing that any return to her former life was now impossible, and unable to see a way to any other.

When her child Hermione came running into the chamber to tell her of the bad dreams that had troubled her sleep, Helen could scarcely bring herself to speak. Filled with self-loathing, she longed for nothing more than to be free of the child for a few hours more and be clasped back in her lover's arms again. But she cast about for words of comfort and promised Hermione that her father would indeed be back in Sparta soon and would keep her safe from all her fears.

Of all the people around her, only one observed the change in Helen that day. Aethra, the former Queen of Troizen who had been her bond-servant and companion for many years, divined at once the agitation of her heart. It was her keen eye that observed the swift change in the colour of her face when Paris appeared in the reception chamber later that morning. And after Helen had vanished for hours that afternoon only to return flustered and distraught, her hair fallen and tangled like a storm-blown vine, it was Aethra, patiently waiting for her in the royal apartment, who looked up from her stitch-work and asked. 'So has the Trojan been thunderstruck by your beauty as my son once was?'

Helen saw at once that there was no point in denial. On the contrary, she felt an overwhelming surge of relief that here was someone with whom she could share the collisions of joy and fear in her heart – though her breath was shaking as she spoke.

'Paris loves me,' she heard herself say. 'Other men's eyes are arrested by this curse. He sees through it to the person beyond. If there were not countless other reasons, I would love him for that alone. And I do love him, Aethra. With Paris, I feel that I know who I truly am. I feel free to be myself.'

'As you do not with the husband who also loves you?'

Helen felt all the pain of the question and was amazed to find it far from mortal. 'I see now,' she answered, 'that I love Menelaus much as I would a friend. A good friend, the dearest friend I have, and, yes, as a good father to my child. And I know very well that is not how he loves me, and my heart grieves for it. But my love for Paris is of another order.' Helen looked up into Aethra's searching gaze, and a wistful smile broke like light across her face. 'For the first time I utterly understand why Penelope refused to give herself to anyone but Odysseus. She was always far braver than me. She was prepared to live alone if need be, rather than foreswear the honesty of her heart. And she was right. I'm only just beginning to realize how much of my own life I have mortgaged to fear. And I'm still afraid, but I believe that Paris's love is stronger than my fear. He has brought me from hiding, out into the elements where I can feel the wind on my face, where I can feel the fire burning under the earth. Aethra, there can be no going back on this.'

'So what will you do?' Aethra asked. 'Does he too mean to carry you away?'

Helen studied the bond-servant's regal face — a face which, many years earlier, had been ignited into life by a single night in the myrtle-grove at Troizen; a face in which a lifetime of womanly suffering through all the long years since was written clearly along the care-lines gouged into her skin. And when Helen spoke, it was as if in answer to a different question.

'But if I go,' she said, 'I go freely this time.'

Aethra considered the needle in her hand. 'Then you are decided?'

'Yes . . . No . . . I don't know.' Helen rocked like a logan-stone on her uncertainty. 'There are so many things that argue against it. Hermione is terrified of Paris. Can I abandon her in Aphrodite's service as my own mother long ago abandoned me for Zeus? Yet if I force her to come with me it will break her father's heart.'

'You have done that already,' Aethra said, 'though he does not know it yet.'

'I know it. Menelaus will go mad with grief when he learns of this.' Helen averted her mind from the thought. 'And I have my duties here . . . I am queen and priestess in Sparta . . . Aethra, what should I do, what should I do?'

'Why do you ask me,' Aethra said quietly, 'when you already know what you will do.' She looked up from the embroidery-frame again. 'Is it not so?'

'It is – may the gods help me,' Helen gasped, 'for they have given me this fate.' And because she could scarcely bear the gently complicit smile of reproach and understanding in the other woman's eyes, she turned her face away.

Then had come the difficult encounter with Aeneas, who returned from the chase wanting only to brag of the huge bear he and his comrades had hunted down. He was showing Paris the shaggy yardage of its skin, to which skull and claws were still attached, with its great maw wrinkled in a snarl, when his distracted friend begged him to be still for a moment and listen.

Secretly placed to overhear them, Helen waited, scarcely breathing throughout the long silence that followed Paris's frank confession of his love for her. Then she was appalled to hear the incredulous, heated oaths and insults that Aeneas heaped on her lover's head, and the merciless accuracy of the questions he shot at him, barb after barb, like arrows from his hunting-bow.

Impassively, Paris withstood it all, answering each question with a grim candour that sought neither exculpation nor extenuation, merely a simple acceptance of the agonizing fact that his love for Helen was such that he was left with no choice but to betray their friend and host by stealing away with his wife.

'Has that Spartan witch driven you out of your mind?' Aeneas demanded. 'Have you forgotten why we came here? Our purpose was to work for peace, not to start a needless war. Get hold of yourself! Think what your father will say to this.'

'I have my father's authority,' Paris answered, though with less certainty.

'To do what? Certainly he once spoke of making off with an Argive woman as hostage to exchange for Hesione if all else failed. But give my body to the dogs if he was thinking of Helen!'

Aeneas was shaking with frustrated rage. 'And all has not yet failed. Our mission is scarcely even begun. Menelaus means to help our negotiations with his brother. He must be preparing the ground right now in Crete.' Aeneas glared at his friend, wide-eyed. 'Or do you mean to betray your city as well as your friend? Would you set all the hosts of Argos against the walls of Troy for the sake of playing at love with a faithless woman?'

Then the two men were arguing so violently that Helen was terrified that someone else – Eteoneus in particular – must also overhear them. She stood trembling in her secret place as the friends all but came to blows.

'We should stop now,' Paris said at last, 'before something is said that cannot be forgiven or forgotten between us. Aeneas, you are my friend and I love you, but in this matter, believe me, my choice is made. I am no longer free to act as though it were not the case. The only question is, are you with me or against me? Whether you like it or not, you too must choose.'

Out of the tense silence of the private chamber, Helen heard the hoarse whisper of Aeneas's voice. 'Menelaus saved my life.'

'I know,' Paris answered, 'I know he did.'

'And this is how you would have me repay him?'

'I would have you do only what you must – even though my life is in your hands.'

'Come away with me now,' Aeneas urged. 'Leave the woman here. Get clear of her for a time. There is a gorge I know in the mountains where you can stand under a fall of melt-water and clear your senses. We will hunt together, and I swear not to speak a word unless it has to do with game or shelter or our life on the crags. Take time to think, and if, after a night or two in mountain air, your feelings remain the same, then I promise to do everything I can to help you.'

But when he looked up he saw his friend smiling so sadly at him that there was scarcely any need for Paris to utter the single, imperative syllable, 'Choose.'

*   *   *

The flight from the palace that night was covert and hasty, though it proved, in the event, less perilous than they feared. One of the attendants who had accompanied the Trojan princes to Sparta left the city openly on horseback in the early evening with secret instructions for the sailing-masters to ready the ships. As soon as the palace was asleep, others were sent to yoke the horses to the chariots and load them with the small amount of baggage that Paris allowed. Most of his own possessions were left behind to make room for Helen's needs, along with those of Aethra and a trusted handmaid, Phylo, both of whom were to flee Sparta with her.

Having made the choice and committed herself, Helen astonished Paris by her cool practicality. Though he assured her that Troy would provide all the wealth she could ever want, she insisted that much of the gold in the treasury was her rightful legacy from her father Tyndareus. The Queen of Sparta was not about to venture out among the hazards of the world without taking the means to provide for her comfort and security. As he watched her filling caskets with gold coins and precious stones, Paris was thinking wryly that, on his return from Crete, Menelaus would find himself lacking more than a wife – a considerable portion of his treasure would have vanished with her too.

It was Helen also who prepared the sleeping draught and mixed it with the jug of wine that Phylo took to the two men guarding the gatehouse that night. But when Paris went to check on the sentries later, he found one of them blearily stirring still. With a prayer to Aphrodite he slit the man's throat, and then, having killed one, he decided – with a ruthlessness that surprised him – that it might be as well to murder the other man too. But on his return to where Aeneas gathered weapons from the armoury, he told him only that the guards were asleep.

An hour had passed since midnight and everything was now in place, yet when Paris went to fetch Helen he found her collapsed in tears, having looked for the last time on her sleeping daughter. Worrying that all his plans must founder on her grief, he pulled her to her feet, whispering, 'Bring the child with you. We will fight our way out if she causes a stir.'

Still contending with her tears, Helen looked up into his gaze as though trying to ascertain whether this man who had over-thrown every stable thing in her life, was a demon or a god.

'You have been brave thus far,' he encouraged her. 'Be braver still. Our life is waiting for you.'

'But it can be won only at terrible cost,' she gasped.

'Yes,' he whispered, and the air between them strummed with that simple acknowledgement of an inescapable truth.

Helen glanced once more at the door of her child's chamber. Then she reached out to grip his arms so tightly that he might have winced at the pain. 'I know I cannot take Hermione with me. It is not her fate. But swear to me you will never forget that I made this sacrifice.'

In the vivid gleam of her eyes he saw the absolute gravity of the demand.

'On my life I swear it,' he whispered.

'Then come,' she said, 'it is time.'

The moon was big still, but its light across the Laconian plain was fitful under the passage of black clouds scudding inland from the sea. Yet only when they were some distance down the hill and out of hearing of the citadel did they climb into the chari-ots and make speed along the river road.

With the wind smarting at her face, and her cloak billowing behind her, Helen stood beside Paris, gripping the chariot rail with white hands while the landscape she had known since birth retreated swiftly around her into the relinquished past. Sparta was gone, Hermione gone, Menelaus gone, and only an uncertain future lay in wait beyond the mountain pass. The wheels jolted at speed along the rough road. Moonlight flashed like molten silver off the horses' backs. As she gulped on air that came at her mouth fast as the torrent of a spring, a surge of exhilaration thrilled through Helen's heart. She was already far gone beyond forgiveness or reprieve, and every fugitive cell of her being felt utterly alive.

There came another death in the mountains. The sentinel on watch at the fastness in the pass was about to call down in challenge when an arrow from Paris's bow took him in the throat. He crumpled at the parapet without a cry.

'That was the first death,' Aeneas muttered grimly within Paris's hearing. 'How many more will have to pay for this?'

But no one else stirred in that small, lax garrison, and minutes later, some four hours after they had crossed the Eurotas river and fled from Sparta, the chariots were through the pass and heading for the port without pursuit.

The ships were already afloat, the crews having been recalled, grumbling, from their various billets in the taverns and stews of the town. Two men who defeated all efforts to find them were left behind to meet whatever fate lay in store for them after the ships weighed anchor and dipped their prows into the swell. As the crew strained at the oar-benches, rain was already falling, cold and sharp, on the deck where Paris watched the greying headland slip away.

It had been agreed that, for safety's sake, the two ships would sail in close company, but as the storm got up and visibility worsened, that proved easier said than done. The whole world was in motion round them, the masthead tilting and plunging, the decks awash, the bow-wave clashing white crests of surf over inky green hollows, the sky a turbid race of blackening cloud. The *Aphrodite* had been toiling among the billows for less than an hour when Helen fell desperately sick.

She lay below decks, groaning in the salt-smell of the bilge, her face white as quicklime, crumpling again and again in drawn grimaces of pain. Out of nervous anxiety, she had eaten almost nothing for hours, and now she was retching on an empty stomach so that only malodorous green bile gushed vilely from her mouth. While Aethra wiped her soiled lips, and Phylo muttered to the sea gods at her side, Paris gathered Helen in his arms, where she panted like a dying dog.

Hours passed without the storm breaking and Helen's condition got no better. Afraid that he had stolen her away from land only to watch her perish at sea, Paris balanced the risk of being overtaken by pursuers against his lover's need to find haven from the turmoil of the storm. When he saw that she had lost even the strength to whisper, he ordered Skopas, his sailing-master, to put in at the first shore he could find.

They fetched up on a small island rising steeply from waters deep enough to risk running their keel into a cove. All around them, a stunned aftermath of fallen rocks lay in gloomy stacks where some casual heave of Poseidon's shoulders had long since scattered them. But the bald hill from which those stones had tumbled huddled its broad back to the storm. There was refuge in its lee.

Paris ordered the awning rigged across the mouth of a cave. A fire was lit from dried-out driftwood and chivvied to a blaze. With his own hand, he made a bed of cloaks and sail-cloth on a slab of rock above a standing pool. Then he carried his lady ashore into the stillness of a place that had, he promised her, never been known to move in a thousand years or more. Filled with love and anxiety, he watched her while she slept.

When he woke she was already bathing in a fall of fresh water deeper inside the cave. At first he thought it dawn, but there was a drenched, lemon glare to the light through the awning and the sky was singed with amber from a westerly sun.

Paris realized that this was still the first day of their flight. They must have slept throughout the afternoon from sheer exhaustion, having travelled all night and been worn out by the turbulence of the sea. But though the swell was still high, the storm had passed, and the woman who walked towards him, drying her slender limbs on a cape, was glistening like a nymph newly minted from the sea. He was famished with hunger and the sharp tang glancing off the briny light made him hungrier still. But his lady was smiling, however wanly. Her spirit was back inside her skin again. And there were other, more urgent appetites to sate.

Kranae – the rocky place – that was the name they gave to the nameless island where, for the first time in freedom, they consecrated themselves to the passion that was Aphrodite's fatal blessing on their lives.

For days, till the seas were calm again, they lived like the survivors of some rich wreck, banishing the others from their sight, feasting on fish and the squid they caught, and diving for sea-urchins, which they stripped back to the orange flesh with knives before swallowing down that vivid taste of sea. Gulls gleamed bright about their heads. The rocks which had once seemed gloomy through the drizzle of the rain were burnished to an ochreous red by sunlight now. They found figs and watermelons on the south-facing terraces of the hill, gasped at the chilly water from its springs, and squeezed the juice of lemons in their hair. They laughed and made love often, both by night and day, and during the drowsy afternoons they shared hot dreams of sleep.

When Skopas complained one morning that his crew grew restless, Paris gave them leave to visit the mainland shore that lay as a grey blur visible across the strait. Taking such store of food and wine as he and Helen might need, he gave orders that the ship return within the week, then the lovers stood together to watch the ship dissolve into the haze.

'And if they should not come back?' Helen said.

'Then we will live here forever,' Paris laughed. 'Here is our kingdom. The island kingdom of Kranae, which has no subjects, no slaves, no history, no worldly ambitions other than to remain itself, and only one law, which is love.'

'Yet we have enemies,' she said.

'Forget them. They will think us far away by now. Come, we will make of this whole island a shrine to the goddess. She is all the protection that we need.'

186

So under the hot sun, on the bare crown of the hill, they gave themselves once more to Aphrodite. And as an excess of wine dissolves the mind into oblivion, it was as if, through a glut of sensuality, they sought to erase from their bodies all memory of a world that must one day make them answer for this dream of liberty.

A Perfect Case for War

In such a manner did Aphrodite, the Golden One, most beautiful and least responsible of goddesses, keep the bargain she had made with Paris on the slopes of Mount Ida when he first discovered that he was far more than the mere herdsman he believed himself to be. Yet the older I have grown and the more I have witnessed of the troubles in the world, the more clearly have I come to see that the gods never fulfil the desires of our hearts without exacting a price for such favour – a price that often proves much heavier than expected. Thus it was that, already, some time before Paris and Helen rejoiced together in the realm of the senses on rocky Kranae, events elsewhere were charged with the far-reaching consequences of their defection into love.

More than two hundred miles across the sea from Sparta, in the sweltering heat of the bull-arena outside the House of the Axe at Knossos on the island of Crete, Menelaus was bestowing prizes at his grandfather's funeral games when the appalling news was brought to him.

The runner who had arrived sweating from the port was troubled by more than the heat. He waited anxiously while the chamberlain whispered in the ear of the Cretan king. Frowning at the interruption, Deucalion nodded and turned to Menelaus who was warmly congratulating the lissom bull-dancer into whose hands he had just thrown an opal ring. 'A ship has put in from Sparta,' he said. 'It seems someone has come with news. He wishes to speak privately with you'

Deucalion had been king in Knossos for more than thirty years now. It was he who had rebuilt the ancient palace of Minos after the labyrinth had been left in ruins by earthquake and the war with Theseus. But the power of Crete was a shade of what it had been for a thousand years before that evil time, and Deucalion felt far from easy that the death of one of his vassals should have brought the sons of Atreus to the island. It had once been among his ambitions to wed his son Idomeneus to Helen of Sparta, and thereby forge an alliance that would strengthen Crete against the growing might of Mycenae. But that hope had failed, so he had been forced to sit with Menelaus beaming at his side, while that crass bully Agamemnon cut a swathe through the palace-women, dreaming of a day when the whole of Crete might lie beneath his sway.

Deucalion caught the briskly disguised flicker of anxiety in his guest's face as Menelaus apologized and got up from his seat. Watching from the corner of his eye, he saw him tilt his head impatiently to catch the whispered message and was astounded to see how the colours changed in the King of Sparta's face.

The dense frown drained to a pallid white, then turned a fierce red as blood rushed back to his cheeks. Menelaus released an involuntary gasp, raised a clenched hand from his side and for a moment Deucalion thought he was about to strike the messenger. But the fist halted against the man's glistening shoulder, the fingers opened, and Menelaus was leaning his weight against the Spartan for support. Taking a few moments to gather himself, he shook his head, pushed back his ruddy locks of hair and glanced uneasily at the people near him. Then he uttered a single, sickly, incredulous laugh, and hissed something at the messenger, who took a step backwards, opening his hands in a helpless gesture of self-exculpation. Menelaus dragged the man further aside. There came a further clipped exchange of questions and answers before the uneasy runner pressed a fist to his brow as he bowed and backed quickly away.

Gathering his wits, unseeing, Menelaus seemed at last to remember where he was. Slowly he walked back to Deucalion. Around them the crowd was applauding the arrival of a new team in the bullring, so Menelaus had to wait for the din to die down a little before his voice could be heard.

'Forgive me,' he said, 'you must give me leave.'

Deucalion summoned a solicitous frown. 'Not bad news, I hope?'

'A matter that requires my urgent attention.' Hearing how hoarse his voice was, Menelaus turned abruptly away. 'Forgive me,' he muttered again, and left the stadium through the excited crowd, angrily demanding that his bewildered attendants let him be. The ground felt unstable beneath his feet. He might have been treading the sea's greasy swell. Alone in the dusty street, Menelaus, King of Sparta, stopped, leaning one hand against a tavern wall where someone had written in a wavering scrawl: Clio is a whore. He had to fight the need to vomit.

Two hours later, the sons of Atreus sat together in a private room of the mansion that had been put at their disposal while they sojourned in Knossos. The dark blue walls were painted with a procession of bare-breasted libation-bearers in flounced skirts, whose upraised arms were wreathed with snakes. During the quake that had wrecked much of the city, a crack had torn through their stately progress like a thunderbolt striking the field of irises through which they walked. Some jobbing builder must have been employed to stitch the masonry together again, but the repair had been painted over with a less costly blue. The chamber still stank of some cloying incense that had been burning there when they first arrived in Knossos. Outside, the sky was gravid with a storm that would not break and the light lent a lurid glow to the yellow blossoms dangling at the casement.

A big man, whose coarsely-haired chest was exposed under the loose gown he had slipped on to cover his nakedness, Agamemnon waited for the slave to set down the wine and leave the room before he spoke again. When he did so, it was in a low, throaty growl.

'The runner was sure about this?'

'He had it from Eteoneus. The words were exact. There can be no doubt.'

Agamemnon nodded. Preferring not to consider the raw evidence around the rims of his brother's eyes, he shifted his gaze about this unsavoury room with a casual indolence that belied the speed of his thoughts.

'Perhaps Eteoneus has got it wrong,' he said. 'The Trojan could have made off with her against her will. He might be holding her hostage for Hesione. I'm surprised Priam hasn't tried it before. It's what I would have done in his place.'

'Do you think I haven't considered that?' Menelaus snapped. 'It was my first thought – once I could begin to believe that this thing had happened at all. But there was no sign of struggle, no disarray in her chamber. Her favourite clothes and jewels are gone. And so is Aethra, and a body-servant she's particularly fond of. And if they had been mere brigands, out for what they could get, they could have forced my whole damned treasury! As it is, Eteoneus thinks she's taken only what she regards as her own.'

'How much would that be?'

Menelaus scowled across at his brother in disbelief. 'Do you think I give a fig for the money when all the light of my life has been put out?' He got up from his couch and crossed to the window where he looked down into the courtyard of the neighbouring mansion. A crate of quails had fallen from the tail of a wagon there and a number of giggling women were chasing the birds about the yard as they panicked on clipped wings.

'Then let's assume,' Agamemnon was saying, 'that your wife has proved wanton enough to run off with this Trojan friend of yours. What do you propose to do about it?'

Menelaus ran a hand through his hair. It came to rest at the back of his neck, which he gripped fiercely in his palm. 'I've already sent orders back to Sparta. They're to double the number of ships scouring the Aegean for them.' His neck and hands were sweating, his eyes closed. 'But they had a whole night's start – and that was three days ago. They could be in Troy long before we have sight of them.' His voice began to shake again. 'It's hopeless!'

Agamemnon snorted impatiently. 'Are you a son of Atreus or a lovesick swain? Pull yourself together, man, or you'll be the laughing-stock of all Crete!' He drew in his breath in a derisive sigh. 'Didn't I tell you that no good would come of fraternizing with these swindling Asiatics? They're about as trustworthy as a pool of crocodiles!'

Menelaus was as consumed by the appalling justice of the remark as he was mortified by it. When he failed to answer, Agamemnon shrugged *out another carefully considered, equally disdainful question. 'In any case, do you really want that Spartan bitch back after she's put a pair of horns on you bigger than any you saw in the ring today?'*

This was too much. Menelaus turned on his brother, furiously red-faced. 'One more insult like that,' he snarled, 'and I'll cut your gizzard open and thrust it back down your throat!'

'That's better, that's better!' Agamemnon smiled. 'If you've been given horns, learn to use them. Rage is what you need. Good, clean, honest, dangerous rage! Enough rage to chase that handsome bastard all the way to Troy if you have to. Enough rage to knot his tripes round his wind-pipe and throw his balls to the dogs! And if you won't do it, I will. No one pisses on the House of Atreus and lives long enough to brag of it.'

'I can take my own vengeance,' Menelaus hissed.

'So it's not hopeless after all,' Agamemnon nodded, smiling. 'Telamon will be there for us. And don't I recall that our wily friend Odysseus got half the princes of Argos to swear some grisly oath before Poseidon that they would fight to defend your right to Helen?'

Agamemnon arched a thick eyebrow at Menelaus, who stood across the room, still trembling a little, clenching and unclenching his fists. Then he took a swig from his wine-cup, relaxed back on his couch, and chuckled. 'The Trojans may think they've got themselves a trophy, little brother. What they've actually got themselves is war!'

And of the dreadful course of the war at Troy and the havoc it wreaked among countless lives, I Phemius, bard of Ithaca, will shortly come to tell.

Glossary of Characters

DEITIES

Aphrodite	Goddess of many aspects, mostly associated with Love and Beauty
Apollo	God with many aspects, including Prophecy, Healing, Pestilence and the Arts
Ares	God of War, twin brother of Eris
Artemis	Virgin Goddess of the Wild
Athena	Goddess with many aspects, including Wisdom, Power and Protection
Boreas	God of the North Wind
Eris	Goddess of Strife and Discord, twin sister to Ares
Eros	God of Love, son of Aphrodite
Ganymedes	Cup-bearer to Zeus
Hephaestus	God of fire and craftsmanship
Hera	Goddess Queen of Olympus, wife of Zeus, presides over marriage
Hermes	God with many aspects, including eloquence, imagination, invention. A slippery fellow
Isis	Egyptian goddess
Nereus	Sea-god

Osiris	Egyptian god
Poseidon	God with many aspects, ruler of the Sea, Earthquakes and Horses
Zephyrus	God of the West Wind
Zeus	King of Olympus, ruler of the gods

MORTALS

Acamas	Argive warrior
Acastus	King of Iolcus
Achilles	son of Peleus and Thetis, leader of the Myrmidons, father of Pyrrhos
Actor	King of the Myrmidons, father-in-law of Peleus, father of Eurytion and Polymela
Adrestos	Trojan warrior
Aeacus	King of Aegina, father of Peleus and Telamon
Aegisthus	son of Thyestes, cousin to Agamemnon and Menelaus
Aeneas	Prince of the Dardanians
Aethra	mother of Theseus, once Queen of Troizen, now bondswoman to Helen
Agamemnon	son of Atreus of Mycenae, High King of Argos
Agelaus	foster-father of Paris, herdsman
Aias	Locrian captain
Ajax	son of Telamon, cousin of Achilles
Alexander	another name for Paris, son of Priam
Anchises	King of the Dardanians
Andromache	wife of Hector
Antenor	counsellor to Priam
Anticlea	mother of Odysseus, wife of Laertes
Antilochus	son of Nestor
Antiphus	son of Priam
Antheus	son of Antenor and Theano
Automedon	charioteer to Achilles and Patroclus

Briseis	Dardanian maiden captured by Achilles
Cadmus	founder of Thebes and husband of Harmony
Calchas	Trojan priest of Apollo who defects to the Argives
Capys	son of Priam
Catreus	grandfather of Agamemnon and Menelaus
Cassandra	daughter of Priam
Cebren	healing priest of Apollo at Sminthe
Cheiron	King of the Centaurs
Chryseis	daughter of Apollo's priest in Thebe, captive of Agamemnon
Cilla	sister of Priam
Cinyras	King of Cyprus
Clymene	Andromache's serving woman
Clytaemnestra	daughter of Tyndareus & Leda, wife of Agamemnon
Cretheis	wife of King Acastus
Cycnus	Trojan hero
Danae	mother of Perseus
Dardanians	people of the Idaean mountains (Dardania), a kingdom of Troy
Deidameia	daughter of King Lycomedes, mother of Pyrrhos by Achilles
Deiphobus	son of Priam
Deucalion	King of Crete, father of Idomeneus
Diomedes	Lord of Tiryns, Argive hero
Diotima	wise woman on Ithaca
Dromeus	Cretan legate
Electra	daughter of Agamemnon & Clytaemnestra
Epeius	Phocian craftsman, designer of the Wooden Horse
Euhippe	Centaur healer & midwife

Europa	mother of King Minos
Eurytion	son of King Actor of the Myrmidons
Eteoneus	chief minister of Sparta
Harmony	wife of Cadmus
Harpale	Dolopian priestess and companion of Thetis
Hector	eldest son of Priam
Helen	daughter of Tyndareus/Zeus and Leda. Queen of Sparta, wife of Menelaus.
Heracles	Greek hero
Hermione	daughter of Menelaus and Helen
Hesione	daughter of Laomedon, sister of Priam
Hippolyta	Amazon queen and beloved companion of Theseus
Hippolytos	son of Theseus and Hyppolyta
Icarius	brother of Tyndareus, father of Penelope
Idaeus	Trojan herald
Idomeneus	son of Deucalion, King of Crete
Iphighenaia	daughter of Agamemnon & Clytaemnestra
Iolaus	charioteer to Heracles
Isus	bastard son of Priam
Jason	Greek hero
Laertes	Lord of Ithaca, father of Odysseus
Laocoon	Trojan priest of Apollo, son of Antenor
Laomedon	King of Troy, father of Priam
Leda	wife of Tyndareus, mother of Clytaemnestra and Helen
Lycaon	son of Priam
Lycomedes	King of Skyros
Machaon	head surgeon in the Argive camp
Memnon	Trojan ally, leader of the Ethiopians

Menestheus	King of Athens
Menelaus	King of Sparta, husband of Helen
Menoetius	bastard son of King Actor, father of Patroclus
Nauplius	King of Euboea, father of Palamedes
Neoptolemus	son of Achilles, also known as Pyrrhos
Nereids	fifty daughters of the sea-god Nereus
Nestor	King of Pylos
Oenone	nymph of Apollo's shrine at Sminthe, daughter of Cebren
Odysseus	Lord of Ithaca
Orestes	son of Agamemnon and Clytaemnestra
Palamedes	Prince of Euboea
Pandarus	Trojan archer
Paris	son of Priam, also known as Alexander
Patroclus	son of Menoetius, beloved friend of Achilles
Peleus	son of King Aeacus, father of Achilles
Penelope	daughter of Icarius, cousin to Helen and Clytaemnestra and wife of Odysseus
Penthesileia	Queen of the Amazons
Pirithous	King of the Lapiths, friend of Theseus
Phaedra	wife of Theseus
Phemius	bard of Ithaca
Phereclus	Trojan shipbuilder
Philoctetes	Aeolian archer
Phocus	son of King Aeacus, half-brother to Peleus and Telamon
Phoenix	Myrmidon warrior
Phylo	handmaid to Helen
Podarces	son of Laomedon, also known as Priam
Polydamna	wise woman to Helen
Polydorus	son of Priam
Polymela	daughter of King Actor, first wife of Peleus

Polyxena	daughter of Priam
Priam	son of Laomedon, King of Troy, also known as Podarces
Prylis	Lapith farrier
Pyrrhos	son of Achilles and leader of the Myrmidons. Also known as Neoptolemus
Sarpedon	Lycian soldier, ally of Troy
Sinon	cousin to Odysseus
Talthybius	Argive herald
Tantalus	King of Elis, first husband of Clytaemnestra
Telemachus	son of Odysseus and Penelope
Telamon	son of King Aeacus, brother to Peleus and King of Salamis. Father to Ajax
Telephus	King of the Mysians and bastard son of Heracles, ally of Troy
Terpis	father of Phemius the Ithacan bard
Teucer	stepbrother to Ajax
Theano	high priestess of Athena in Troy, wife of Antenor
Thersander	friend of Diomedes and commander of the Boeotians
Thersites	Argive soldier and kinsman of Diomedes
Theseus	hero, King of Athens, conqueror of Crete
Thetis	daughter of Cheiron, second wife of Peleus and mother of Achilles
Thyestes	brother to Atreus of Mycenae, uncle to Agamemnon and Menelaus. Father of Aegisthus
Thymoetes	son of Priam
Tithonus	King at Susa, half-brother of Priam
Tyndareus	King of Sparta, father of Clytaemnestra and Helen, husband of Leda
Typhaon	Dragon

Acknowledgements

The guidance of Robert Graves' classic work of reference, *The Greek Myths, is* evident everywhere throughout this book, and I would have been lost without his patient and imaginative scholarship. Though I have tried to remain faithful to the broad outlines of the stories as Graves records them, I have not hesitated to license my own, often anachronistic, imagination wherever I felt it necessary. Having no Greek, I was also heavily dependent on the majestic verse translations of Homer's *Iliad* made by Richmond Lattimore and Robert Fagles, and on the lively prose version composed by E.V. Rieu. Jules Cashford's fine English versions of the Homeric Hymns were also an invaluable pointer to the power and beauty of the culture behind these myths. I found Michael Wood's *In Search of the Trojan War* to be an engagingly readable guide to the archaeology of Troy and Mycenae, and Mary Renault's marvellous novels *The King Must Die* and *The Bull from the Sea* were a constantly challenging inspiration.

More personally, I wish to acknowledge the help and encouragement given to me by my editor Jane Johnson, by my agent Pat Kavanagh, and by my family and friends, particularly Elspeth Harris, Stephen Russell and James Simpson. Also I owe a big round of thanks to the Happy Hour crowd at the Milk Street

200

Brewery for keeping my spirits up and my wits sharp. The deepest debt, however, is to my wife Phoebe Clare for bearing with me and for asking more of the book and its author than either would have found on their own.